Two Boys a Dog and an Old Man

By Guy Ignafol

Life has a way of bringing people and events together. Family, friends, young and old, cross paths in ways that are difficult to explain.

Much appears to be by coincidence or consequence, of the gift of choice we have been given, by our creator.

The boundaries of breath and body and needs for sustaining life limit our access to the glory of our eternal life.

It is my belief that these are the tools, used in eternity by spirit, with no boundaries.

It is an attempt to show life, and its boundaries. And share faith and hope in a world that is limited and influenced by events that are out of our control, to serve the creator in our eternal life.

Our Father, which art in heaven,
Hallowed be thy Name.
Thy Kingdom come.
Thy will be done in earth,
As it is in heaven.
Give us this day our daily bread.
And forgive us our trespasses,
As we forgive them that trespass against us.
And lead us not into temptation,
But deliver us from evil.
For thine is the kingdom,
The power, and the glory, For ever and ever.
Amen.

The Brothers

There was a mother and a father, Benny and Barb, who had twin sons. The boys looked so much alike that to the passerby, there was no way to tell the difference. But their mother intuitively knew, from some undefinable sense, which was which.

The boys were healthy and smart and caught on to words and colors at a competitive rate, each teaching the other. They could not be separated either in speech or knowledge, sight nor sound. When one learned to write the other intuitively would know the letters, phrases and sentences. They would start a conversation and before the sentence could be completed, the brother would finish.

This had friends, family and acquaintances in awe, and they would, if for no more than the fun of it, pretend to be each other. Normally this would work with precision, but their mother could not be fooled,   She would call them out by name and no matter how they tried to convince her she was wrong, that inner force would tell her who was who, and she would stand her ground until the boys confessed and moved on to the next attempt.

The boys like most, liked to play in the dirt, with trucks tractors and dozers, one digging a hole and the other filling it in. Lincoln logs to build a house and a baseball to knock it down. Picking up the pieces and going through the exercise over and over.

As they got older they would play detective alternating between the good and the bad guy. They loved to read, swapping books on completion and pretending to be the characters they had read about.

Their names were Bill and Bob and soon had been marked as a pair, the BBs'.

When the neighborhood would get the baseball teams together to play, the BBs' would be called out with identical gloves, identical hats, jeans and shoes, no one cared what position either of them played, always knowing they would play fair and their best, and play to win.

The Neighborhood

The boys grew up in a medium sized city with many neighborhoods. They were sectioned off by blocks and if you lived on a block you were from that block, and identified as from that block. If your block had a baseball team it played the team from another block, and if your block came with 8 players and the other block came with 11, you played one man short and the other block had one man sit.

Blocks were blocks and there would be no exceptions win or lose.

The blocks were made of yards and the yards might or might not be fenced. The yards that were not fenced would become public property so a field could be made crossing property lines. This was not an issue within the block, whether you had kids or not, and was well recognized by the worn base paths, home plate being the biggest patch of worn grass.

There were trees, and some of them were of pretty good size. These were recognized as natural obstacles and under no circumstances could be removed for the sake of the field. If the ball was hit into a tree and deflected, it by the rule of fair play would become a ground rule double. No exceptions no arguments. The ground rule double was often used to give your team an edge if there was a man on second or third. Hit it into the tree and you were guaranteed scored runs and a double, causing a lot of chatter but never over-ruled or discussion of sacrificing a tree.

The blocks, and Neighborhoods were well defined. With boundaries recognized by all, as were the inhabitants.

When there was a non-block member in the mix, a block member mom was aware, and if one mom was aware all block member moms would soon be aware.

The 4th Grade

This is where it starts. Billy and Bobby, in school in their assigned seats with no-one knowing if Bob or Bill is in the right seat, or if both of them are, but always in the very back of each of the students and the teachers mind, are we being fooled?

Was this just a passing thought, or is the one called on, more important than the question to be answered.

Do they know we are all wondering who is who; and do they care?

Do they both like Missy or is just one of them pulling her pig-tails?

So school is out and the BBs' are home, on the block in the neighborhood in the back yard playing catch with identical gloves, in identical hats with identical jeans and shoes, no-one but mom knowing which is which.

Fast ball after fast ball, curve after curve, one calling strikes as he catches and after 30 pitches switching from one being the pitcher to being the catcher. Until deciding to take a break, lie down in the grass and stare up into the big tree that had afforded them many ground rule doubles and scoring countless runs.

As they lay in the grass looking up at the tree, mom comes out and asks if they would like some lemonade, and why they were lying in the grass?

"Just taking a break looking at the tree" they said in unison "Lemonade would be great".

And their mom went on her business, going into the house and mixing the lemons with sugar and water and adding ice so it was just perfect for her two boys.

When she finished, she started toward the door and on her way picked up two identical pencils and two identical pads and took the identical glasses of lemonade to identical twin boys and they in unison said thanks mom. "What are the pencils and pads for? "

The mom said, "I would like you to do something for me".

The boys asked, "What?" And the mom said, "I just want you to write down what you see when you look at that tree."

The boys laughed and said, "We see a tree."

Their mom said, "I'm sure you do, but I am also sure that you will see more. I would like you to go into your inner thoughts and write down what you see when you look into that tree. There are a couple of conditions. You must not identify who you are, and you must not let the other read it when you are done. You must lay it face down on the table in the dining room and tell me when you are done. I will collect them, read them and cherish every word. So speak from your inner self just to your mom. And recognize that if you break any of these conditions I will know, I am your mother and I know who is who".

In that the boys looked at each other and laughed. They agreed to the conditions and started looking back up into the tree.

It seemed funny from one brother to the other that neither had started to write, and Bill said to Bob.

"Why aren't you writing?" And Bob said to Bill, "I am looking at the tree differently than I have ever looked at it. This will take some time." They agreed and continued to look up into the tree.

The Tree

The boys never looked at the tree the same way again, but look at it they did. They could not pass by it without having a different thought.

Being the boys they were, they wanted to please their mom and write something that was sure to be cherished, but try as they may the first words could not be brought from pencil to paper.

Their mom would watch the boys as they passed or lay under the tree and see the wheels turning, the pads of paper getting soiled from being carried, and the pencils still as sharp as the day they were presented.

Days turned to nights and nights to days and days to weeks and weeks to months.

Finally one afternoon Bill and Bob came to their mom, and either Bill or Bob said, "This is much more difficult than we first thought. We want it to be just right and would like you to cherish our words. Can you help us?"

The boys' mother smiled and hugged the boys, and said that they could be assured that whatever words they wrote would be cherished. But this was something they must do on their own. She did though have a suggestion that may help.

Tonight boys, when you go to bed and say your prayers, ask God to guide your pencils. If there is one thing in life I am sure of, it is that God is in you, both of you, and he can help you see all that is in that tree to be cherished.

One of the boys said to their mother, "Won't God guide our pencils to say the same thing, if we are to write what will be cherished?"

The mother replied, "He may have some things that you will see the same, but he has made us all different, with the ability to see the world in our own way, and I am certain that he will take that into account as he guides you."

That night, as Benny took his boys upstairs to bed, he asked them if they had a good day and if there was anything they needed to tell their Dad before they said their prayers and went to sleep. The boys thought hard, and said, "No." They got on their knees at the side of the bed and waited for their father to leave the room and close the door to say their prayers.

The boys said their prayers as they did every night, but this night at the end of their prayer, they asked God if he would please guide their pencils to write cherished words about the tree. With renewed confidence they slipped under the covers and went to sleep.

Now Benny was a big Dad and though to this point, he has not been mentioned. He was a very important part of Billy and Bobs' life.

He was not much of a talker but when he said something everyone heard it, and it was loud and clear. No matter if yelled or whispered.

Benny worked hard and his hands showed it. They were leathered on the palm and heavy veined on the back side. His fingers were thick and scarred and coarse to the touch.

But he had a gentle pat when he placed them on top of the boys head.

Every night the Dad would ask the boys if there was anything they needed to tell their Dad before they said their prayers.

This was their opportunity to fess up and let their dad know if they had done anything that day that would bring displeasure to him or the family, get it off their chest, and face the consequences.

Benny was always one to say, "spare the rod and spoil the child," but neither of the boys had ever seen the rod, nor had any desire to; but were aware that the dad had a pad of his own and a pencil with a sharp point, and if the deed was bad enough for him to write it down, it was bad enough not to be repeated.

Make no mistake, boys will be boys and these boys were boys. Broken windows, water hoses left running, bikes left at the neighbors' house, balls thrown in the house with broken vases, and potato fights in the basement.

So the boys woke up the next day with a new lease on describing their vision of the tree.

Days turned to nights and nights to days and days to weeks and the boys every night at the end of their prayers, would ask God to help them guide their pencil to write cherished thoughts about the tree.

Every day they would pass by the tree and look at it, and every day they would see something just a little different, until finally after a few weeks they went back to their mother.

"Mom," they said, "We keep asking God to help guide our pencils and it just isn't happening. We are not sure if we can write what you will about the tree in words that you will cherish."

The mom smiled at her sons and said, "maybe God is not ready to guide your pencils." Maybe he is waiting for you to come to the place in life when you can best write words about the tree that he will cherish. As important as it is to serve your mother, it is of greater importance that you serve God. I know as sure as I am standing here, that when he is ready, he will provide direction.

Keep praying and keep looking at that tree, trust your mother, and trust God.

The Writings

It was a Monday or maybe it was a Wednesday, no matter, it was the day that mom heard the boys' call from upstairs, to look on the dining room table.

The mom went to the closet and pulled a shoe box off the top shelf, and carried it into the dining room.

There sat two sheets of paper face down on the table.

She walked up to the papers and without turning them over folded them twice, with the writing to the inside. Went to the shoe box and pulled out two envelopes, and neatly and gently placed the writings in the envelopes. Sealed them and placed them back in the box. No names were on the sheets and none were put on the envelopes.

From upstairs came a holler, "Did you get them, Mom?"

And from the dining room the mother yelled, "Yes, I have your words, and they will always be cherished. I know they are from your hearts and directed by God and I couldn't be any more pleased than what I am right now".

"Remember these words are between you and me and God. I can't discuss them with you as they are not identified, and you are not to discuss them with each other or anyone else. If you need to talk about it, thank God for the direction, and for providing cherished words."

The boys, knowing that it was important to play fair and follow the rules, accepted that their words would be cherished and that if they needed any confirmation, they should reach out to God in prayer, and he would insure their acceptance.

The Seventh Grade

The brothers were getting big and were smart, handsome and identical. Everyone liked them and they liked everyone.

The fact that they were a little different in being twins, made it easier for them to accept the differences in others. Their circle of friends included those in the book club, on the baseball team, boys and girls of all races and religions and dogs. They loved dogs.

Their father had gifted them with a dog when they had started the 7th grade. The reason for the gift was unique and held a special meaning to the boys.'

It seems that list that was kept by their father was re-started every year on a new sheet. And at the end of the school year of the 6th grade, the father tallied the number of entries, and found that there were between the two of them, only 17 incidents to record.

Boys being boys, and the BBs' certainly being boys, had achieved a record low number of recordable incidents.

So one night when their father took them up to bed and asked if there was anything they needed to talk to him about, and the boys sad "no" the father let them kneel by the side of their bed to pray and left the room. After they had finished their prayer and slipped under the covers, the bedroom door opened slightly, allowing a flash of light and then again darkness.

This was totally out of the ordinary, and Billy said to Bob, "What was that about?" And one or the other turned on the night light.

At the door sat a pup with big eyes and bigger paws and a tail that was wagging like a windshield wiper.

Next to the pup was an envelope, and Billy opened it, while the Bobby picked up the pup.

The note said, "I went to your mother and asked what I could do to show you boys how much I love you, and she told me to ask for direction in my prayers."

"I prayed and prayed but came up with nothing."

I went back to your mother and said I wasn't getting any answer to my prayers. She told me that maybe God was not ready to show me the best way to show my sons how I feel.

"When I was at the store the other day there was a man with a dog and one pup. He told me that he had found a home for all the other pups in the litter. But this one was the runt, and he had no takers."

"My prayer was answered and now I get to share it with my sons. I know it is from my heart, and directed by God, you need say nothing to me; but if you feel blessed, please give your thanks to God."

The next morning after little sleep Billy or Bob took the note down stairs and left it face down on the dining room table.

One or the other yelled down the steps to their mother; "Dad left us a note. Put it somewhere safe for us and we will be down soon. It is on the dining room table face down. We need to show you something."

The boys' mother yelled back up the stairs "I have a perfect spot for it" and she walked to the closet pulled a shoe box from the top shelf, pulled an envelope from it and without turning it over folded the note three times with the writing to the inside, placed the note in the envelope, sealed it, with no markings and no names, put it in the box and back on the top shelf in the closet.

The Dog, an Old Man and the Tree

This was not just a regular dog. Or maybe it was a very regular dog, but certainly it was special to the boys'.

The night the puppy had been left in the room it did as puppies do, whimper and whine and make a mess of things, and the boys cuddled it and pet it and took it to bed with them, none getting much sleep but all enjoying every minute of it.

Stepping out of bed either Billy or Bob walked toward the bathroom and with one step felt something warm and mushy between his toes. With his next step, something cold and wet. And that is how the puppy got his name "Poodles" a combination of poop and puddle. And the boys had a taste of pleasure and pain with ones you love, and cleaned up the mess.

That night, the boys and Poodles met their father at the door. And with his big hands with the leathery palms and thick fingers coarse to the touch, patted the boys on the head and as the boys introduced Poodles, gave him a gentle pat as well.

At dinner the boys and their mother and father with Poodles looking on, went over all the things that would be necessary for the boys to do to make sure that Poodles would fit into the family with as little disruption as possible.

The boys took a sharp pencil and a pad of paper and wrote everything down. They did not want toforget to do all that was necessary to ensure an acceptable environment for all members of the family and for Poodles too.

19

While they were writing down the responsibilities of ownership their father said, "Barb I have twelve years of lists that I need a safe place to keep. Can you think of anything I can do with them?"

Barb said, "When you get done with your dinner bring the lists to the dining room and lay them face down on the table."

So, after dinner, Barb went to the closet and pulled a shoe box from the top shelf, took it to the dining room and took an envelope out for each list, folded the lists neatly with the writing to the inside, placed each one neatly in its own envelope and sealed them. No identification, no names, and placed them in the box and placed the box on the top shelf in the closet.

"Poodles" was sweet, and he was loved, and loving, and just smart enough without being too smart. He learned fast and before long the boys had him trained to go outside to do his business. He could sit, speak, and when he was hungry, he would pick up his bowl and bring it to one of the boys to fill.

This being quite rewarding, his motivation was not always hunger as everyone thought that he was so cute for doing such a thing.

The boys put a harness on Poodles and would walk him every day when they got home from school. This was a big event for Poodles, and he soon learned to pick up his leash and bring it to the boys as a reminder.

On one of the days and one of the walks with Poodles, the boys dressed in the same shoes and the same jeans and the same caps came upon an old man walking down the street in the opposite direction.

The old man stopped in front of the boys and said, "That's quite a dog you have there, what's his name?"

The boys replied, "Poodles."

The old man said, "No you boys don't understand, I didn't ask what kind of dog it was, I asked what his name was. Besides that doesn't look like any poodle I have ever seen".

The boys looked at each other and then at the old man and said, "We named him Poodles".

The old man was like many older men, becoming more curious in this encounter as the conversation went on. And he saw an opportunity to share some wisdom with the two boys.

"Ok, "the old man said. "The dogs' name is "Poodles". But being he doesn't look like a poodle, what kind of dog is he?"

Again the boys looked at each other and said, "Dad told us he was a "Runt".

The old man laughed and said, "So Poodles is a "Runt," and how did this "Runt" get the name, Poodles?"

"Well, one of us got up in the morning and stepped in some poop, and then we stepped in some pee," they replied.

This made the old man raise an eyebrow and said, "So one of you stepped in a pile of dog poop and then in a puddle of pee and named your dog Poodles"

"Exactly," the boys said.

"Can you give me a little better understanding of how this came about?" asked the Old Man.

"Sure," said the boys, "Our dad wanted to give something special for doing 17 bad things. He keeps a list, and we tell him all the bad things we do when we go to bed. He always says, "Spare the rod and spoil the child."

He asked my mom what he should give us for doing 17 bad things, and she told him to pray about it. So he did and God sent him to the store. There was a man that had a "Runt" that he didn't want, so God told my dad to give it us for doing the 17 bad things.

The boys looked at each other and nodded, feeling that this had been a pretty fair description of events.

"So let me get this straight," said the old man. "God told your father to give you a runt dog, for doing 17 bad things, and you named him Poodles because you stepped in a pile, and some pee".

"Yes," said the boys, "Poodles is a combination of poop and puddle, and it seemed to fit".

The old man became more curious on every word from the boys.

"So," said the old man, "What if you had done 16 bad things? What would your father have given you?"

"Well, we have never done 16 bad things, so we don't know".

"And if had you done 18 bad things?" said the old man.

The boys looked at each other again tilted their heads, and said, "we have done 18 bad things before."

"And what did you receive for those 18 bad things?" asked the Old man.

"Nothing," said the boys.

By this time the old man was questioning his wisdom, and studied the boys up, down, and side-ways, and the dog too.

"What are your names boys?" asked the old man, with a tilted head and one closed eye.

"Billy and Bob," said the boys, "People call us the BBs'."

"Hmm the BBs'," said the old man. I notice that you have the same shoes, the same jeans, and the same caps on. How can people know which one is Billy and which one is Bob?"

"Most people can't," said the boys, "but our mom knows."

"And how would it be that your mother knows and no-one else can tell?" asked the old man.

The boys had always been told not to talk to strangers, and this conversation was getting pretty deep, so one of the boys held up one hand with his index finger to the sky. Requesting the man wait, as they turned around took two steps and had a brother to brother conference.

After agreeing that the old man was very nice and that they enjoyed answering his questions, they turned back toward him, and took two steps forward to their original places.

"Well, one day she had us look at a tree and told us that she knew which of us was which."

"A tree," the old man said.

"Yes," said the boys, "a tree."

"And was there something special about this tree?" asked the old man.

"Oh yes," said the boys, "but we didn't know it the first time we looked at it."

"And how many times did you have to look at the tree?" said the old man.

"Many times," said the boys, "Mom gave us a pad of paper and pencil and told us to write down what we saw when looked at the tree."

"So, you looked at this tree and wrote down what you saw, on a pad of paper, with a pencil your mother gave you. And that is how your mother knows which of you is which."

"And, how often would you look at this tree before you knew what to write?" said the old man.

"All the time, we looked and looked at it for days and days and weeks and weeks and couldn't decide what to write on the paper. So we asked our mother to help us."

24

"So your mother told you what to write about the tree?" said the old man.

"No", said the boys. "We each wrote about the tree and put what we wrote face down on the dining room table when we got it done. Mom said we couldn't put our names on it."

"So your mother wouldn't help you and you didn't put your names on the sheets of paper. You didn't know what to write on the paper and you put the papers on a table without your names, and your mother knows which of you wrote the descriptions of the tree," said the old man.

The boys both tilted their heads the same way, brought their lower lip over their upper lip and nodded "Yes" to confirm the statement.

"So, how did you know what to write on the paper?" asked the old man.

"We prayed about it and when God thought it was the right time he guided our pencils" said the boys.

"And what did God guide your pencils to say?" asked the old man.

"We can't tell you," said the boys.

"Did God say you couldn't tell me?" said the old man.

"No," said the boys, "Mom did."

"What did you think of what your brother wrote?" asked the old man.

25

"I don't know" said one of the boys, "never read it and can't tell him."

"And was this directed to you by God or by your mother?" said the old man.

"God didn't say anything to us about it, just Mom. Not sure if he talked to her about it. She never said."

By this time the old man felt like he had absorbed about all he could from the conversation. He told the boys that it had been a pleasure to talk to them, and would look forward to seeing them again. The boys nodded and told the old man they enjoyed talking to him also, and would look for him, on their walks with the dog.

Growing Up

The boys were getting to an age where their interests were expanding and their involvement in school activities and sports varied. Most of the time though they would follow each other's path, they seemed to find comfort in doing things together, it built their confidence and helped to keep them in check as they took on daily events. It also helped to keep the numbers down on their Fathers' list.

This however did not have an effect on their relationship with Poodles, or interfere with their daily walks. Poodles would not let them forget. The leash in his mouth reminded the boys of the walk that was so eagerly awaited by their trusted friend.

In the summer and on the weekends, Poodles knew when the normal time passed for them to get up and that it was his task to collect the leash and roust the boys from bed. This meant for an early walk and a special moment for the boys before they took on their day.

For some odd reason, every day as they took their walk, they would encounter the old man.

Some days there would be conversation but usually the old man would walk straight up, bend over and pet Poodles, and ask' "Have either of you stepped in a pile or puddle that morning?" Smile and walk away. Sometimes as he walked away he would tell them not to take any wooden nickels. The boys had no idea what this meant but always envisioned a wooden nickel with a buffalo on one side and an Indian head on the other. Often they would laugh as they walked away; not at the old man, but because they were happy to have had the encounter.

This was not his only greeting, "You keeping the numbers up on your dad's list? Does your mom still know which is which, or do you need to write down what you see in a blade of grass?" Never did he miss petting Poodles on the head and rubbing him behind the ears. It was hard to tell if he enjoyed seeing the boys or the dog more. But it would certainly be apparent to any passer-by that it was a highlight of the day, not only to Poodles, but to the Old man and the boys.

One day the Old man stopped and as they were going through their daily ritual, asked the boys if they would be able to come by his house and help him with a couple of chores that were a little more than he was able to handle.

The boys were unsure about committing to this without talking to their parents. Said so to the old man, and told him they would like to, but would have to get back to him.

They really liked the old man and the thought went through both of their minds that it might hurt his feelings if they told him the reasoning.

As though he knew their thoughts the old man said, "If you would like me to talk to your parents about it, I would gladly do so. I would want them to feel comfortable with you being with me at my house." The boys asked if they could bring the dog and the old man said with a smile, "If you can't bring him maybe you shouldn't come. You're kind of a team."

The boys went home and talked to their Mother and Dad, and told them that they had a friend that had a house and that he had asked them to come over and help him with a few things. That they would like to do so and, "Would it be ok?"

The boys had kind of a way of asking for permission by the way they saw the situation. Both Mother and Father decided to delve a little deeper into the request.

"Where did you meet this friend?" asked their mother.

"On our walks," said the boys.

"What is his name" said the father.

"Don't know," said the boys.

"Where does he live?" asked their mother.

"Don't know," said the boys.

"He really likes Poodles," said the boys.

"How did it come up that this friend of yours asked you to come to his house?" asked their Father.

The boys could see where this conversation was going, and as much as they liked the old man, and as comfortable as they were with him, their parents had some serious concerns. This seemed like the perfect time to tell them that their friend had told them that he would be glad to meet their parents, so all would feel comfortable with the situation. So they did.

The boys' parents said, they thought this was a good idea and would look forward to meeting their friend on Saturday. Dad would not be working and sure to be home and their mother would, if the boys wanted, make lunch.

The next day the boys took their walk and when they came upon the old man, told him their mom and dad would like to meet him.

The old man said, "It would be a pleasure. When would be a good time?"

Mom said Dad would be home on Saturday and that she would make lunch, "is there anything special you would like to have to eat?"

The old man thought for a minute and said, "I can't imagine not liking anything that you boys like. You decide and I am sure it will be very good. Tell your parents I am looking forward to meeting them."

Before the boys walked on they said, "We will meet you here on Saturday at noon. We can walk to our house together."

The Old man thought that was a good idea and said so, being he had no idea where the boys lived. As he walked away he said, "Don't take any wooden nickels." The boys assured him they would not, laughed, and went on their way.

Saturday morning came and the boys' mother asked if their friend was still planning to come.

The boys said, "Yes."

The boys' mother asked if he would be joining them for lunch, and if so. "Was there anything special that he might like?"

The boys said, "We asked him and he told us that he would like what we like."

"Poodles" was a bit confused as he had taken his leash to the boys and being Saturday there seemed to be a delay in their departure. Time passed and the boys clipped the leash to the harness and off they went.

As they walked, as was normal, they came across the Old man. He approached them head on, and bent over to pet Poodles and patted him on the head.

The boys turned around and said, "Mom is getting lunch ready and Dad will eat with us. It's not far just a couple of blocks."

The boys walked and talked as they normally did with the old man, but this was the first time they had talked with him while walking. They noticed their pace had slowed and Poodles had taken position next to the Old man, adjusting their speed.

As they came to the house they passed the walk to the front door and walked up the drive to side, of the house. This was their normal way of entry. Before they opened the door, they unleashed Poodles. The door opened and Poodles ran in with the boys and the Old man following.

There was a reason behind this sequence of events. The boys never used the front door. Poodles, for safety sake always entered first, and when the boys came in the house, the shoes came off.

This was no different than any other time, so after entering the house the boys removed their shoes. The old man took notice and removed his, revealing a big toe exposed by a hole in his sock.

The kitchen was set right off the back door, and when the boys and the Old man entered the father was seated at the head of the table and the Mother was standing at kitchen sink.

The table was set neatly with 3 glasses of milk, two cups of coffee and 5 paper plates, 5 bowls of Macaroni and Cheese and a platter of hot dogs, with ketchup and mustard in a squirt bottles and relish. There were celery sticks with peanut butter and raisins on top, and one cookie at each setting, on a napkin of its own, for dessert.

The boys' father was somewhat taken aback when the old man entered the room and abruptly stood up out of respect.

"Welcome," the father said, and held out his hand to shake the hand of the old man.

"A working man," said the old man in a complimentary manner. "I can tell by the hands".

"Yes," said the father with pride.

"Oh, yes. Welcome; said the boys' mother. "The boys said you would like what they like for lunch; I hope this will be ok."

"Hot dogs, macaroni and cheese, and ants on a log, looks good to me," said the Old man, "Oh, and a cookie."

"I have coffee if you like," said the mother.

The father gestured for the Old man to take a seat.

"Thought this glass of milk might be for me," said the old man as he sat down.

"It is," said the mother, "but if you would prefer I can pour you a cup."

"Milk goes good with hot dogs and cookies; I think this will be just perfect."

The boys sat down and smiled. They were pleased that the Old man would like his lunch.

The father took notice that Poodles took a place next to the old man, lying with his head on his paws. The old man without thinking reached down and patted Poodles on the head.

The father asked the boys if they would like to say prayers, and the Old man spoke up and asked if it would be ok if he did the honors.

"Of course," said the mother.

All bowed their heads and closed their eyes.

"God is Great;" said the old man, God is Good. By his hand we all are fed. We thank him for our daily bread. In Jesus name we pray. Amen"

Everyone lifted their heads and opened their eyes. There was a smile on every face. The father picked up the platter of hot dogs and passed them to the left.   The old man first. Taking one and placing it on paper plate, he in turn passing it around and everyone else following suit.

"There is ketchup and mustard for your hot dog," said the boys father.

"Mustard for me and a little relish never was able to make a hot dog with ketchup work for me. I know a lot of people like them that way. I'm just not one of those people."

As everyone dressed their dog, the mother and father noticed their boys put only mustard and relish on theirs. This came as quite a surprise as normally they would put only ketchup on their dog. Neither of them had ever seen them take the mustard and relish route.

"The boys mentioned that you might have something they could help you with," said the father.

"Well actually there are a number of things I need to get done, I have some health issues and I can't do what I used to be able to do."

"I would not be able to pay them, but will certainly make it worth their time and effort. You have fine boys and I would never take advantage of them."

"Where bouts do you live?" asked their mother.

"A few blocks over on Elm Street. You are welcome to come over if you would like to see what needs to be done and where the boys will be. They plan on bringing "Poodles" with them. He's quite the guard dog. I found the origin of his name to very creative."

The father chuckled, "Speaking of names, could I ask yours?"

This came as quite a surprise to the old man. Not because the boys' father wanted to know, but that this was the first that he had realized, that he had never identified himself to the boys.

"Ray," "Ray Johnson," said the old man, "and yours?"

"Benny and Barb Buxton," said the father.

"Benny and Barb Buxton and the BBs, that's a lot of B's. Sounds like a rock and roll band," he replied.

This time everyone chuckled, especially the boys, they had become familiar with the way the old man talked, and knew he felt comfortable with their parents. This had special meaning to them.

As lunch went on, the conversation grew about the relationship the boys had made to Old man.

How he was fascinated by the fact that the boys were rewarded for doing bad things and how the decision was made to get the boys a "Runt" for a gift.

There was no in-depth response other than what had been explained to the old man by the boys, and every time it appeared that it might drift into an uncomfortable area. One of the boys would find a way to interrupt and divert the conversation. What the Old man knew was accurate and told by the boys and in their mind, needed not to be qualified or explained in any greater detail.

Ray, on the other hand, was left curious about lists, trees and writings left on the dining room table.

As Ray finished all but the last bite of his hot dog, he dropped his right hand under Poodles' nose and fed him the bite.

"Oh," said one of the boys. "We don't feed Poodles from the table. We had a special meeting over dinner and wrote down a list of rules to make sure that we could all get along with as little disruption to the others or the house as possible."

"And did Poodles agree to all these rules?" asked the Old man.

"No," said one of the boys. "We have to follow the rules so he doesn't do anything to get himself into trouble."

"Well I feel much better then," said the Old man. "If he didn't know the rule and I didn't know the rule," I will ask you and your family to excuse my lack of manners, and Poodles actions. With a promise, if permitted to read the list, and abide by the written rule. Not only here, but if you boys are allowed to come to my house, abide by them there also."

The boys confirmed that they would provide the list to the old man. And that if there were other rules that needed to be followed, they would add them to the list.

They were willing to sit down and write them, and present the list to their parents and the old man for approval.

"Let's think about this a minute," said the mother. "Your father and I know the rules for Poodles, why don't you boys and Ray sit here at the table. After I clean up you can set the rules for going to Ray's house. When you are done, put the list on the dining room table face down. Be sure and put the list of the rules for the dog with it. If there is a problem with it, your father and I will let you know and you can make adjustments."

The Old man and the boys agreed that this was a reasonable way to make sure that all parties would be considered and that they would start on the list right after lunch.

One of the boys ran upstairs and grabbed the list of the dog rules and laid it next to the ketchup on the kitchen table.

The old man was right, the cookies and milk went well together and were enjoyed by the three friends.

As they wrote the rules for going to the Old man's house they tried to think of everything. One would talk about how long they should be able to stay, before having to call home. One talked about shoes on or off in the house. Bathroom rules, kitchen rules, dog rules, language rules. The three sat and stretched their imaginations, completed the list, and made an extra copy for the Old man.

The original was placed face down on the dining room table.

The boys called to their mother that it had been completed, and she replied, that she would take care of it. Moving, as she spoke toward the closet and reaching on the top shelf for the shoe box, taking it to the dining room, removing an envelope for each list and folding the list twice with the writing to the inside, placing them neatly into their own envelope, placing the envelopes into the box and returning it to the top shelf in the closet.

"Is it all right?" yelled one of the boys from the kitchen.

"I believe between the three of you, all the most important things have been covered," replied the mother. "Follow the rules you have decided on that are on this list, and neither your father or I could ask for anything more."

Going to a Friends' House

It was Wednesday and Poodles had just grabbed the leash and run upstairs. The boys took their showers and got dressed. They went down-stairs to have a quick breakfast and start their walk.

Poodles waited patiently by the door prepared to take on his main event of the day. As the boys approached the door, one turned to their mother and said, "On Saturday we are going to our friends' house. We will be leaving here at 10:00 and will be home by 2:00. If we are going to be any later one of us will call you."

"So you are going to Rays?" their mother asked.

"Yes, we are going to help him clean his garage. He said he would make sure if we were hungry, there would be something to eat."

"Ok, said the boys' mother. "Will Poodles be going too?"

"Yes," replied the boys. And they made off on their walk, with Poodles leading the way.

On their walk the saw the Old man and he approached straight away. He petted Poodles on the head and rubbed behind his ears.

"We talked to mom about Saturday and she is good with it. We will be leaving the house about 10:00 and should be to your house about 10:15."

"That should work out fine." said the Old man. "Did you tell what you would be doing and what time to expect you home?"

"Yes," said one of the boys, "and we told her you would give us lunch if we got hungry".

The old man raised his right hand as if to say all was well, and started to walk away. He then turned back to tell the boys not to take any wooden nickels.

Thursday and Friday being between Wednesday and Saturday, the three of them, with Poodles met up with each other two more times. Their encounters were strangely short, all parties eagerly anticipating Saturday's main event. On Friday though the Old man said, "you're sure you know where my house is?"

The boys replying that they did. And the Old man passing by raising his right hand, and saying, "see you about 10:15."

Saturday arrived and Poodles made his way to the boys' bedroom, leash in mouth, tail wagging. He jumped on the bed and rousted the boys with vigor as if he knew there was something special about the day. The boys rolled out and got their showers taken, brushed their teeth, got dressed, and headed for the kitchen.

"Good morning Mom," they said in unison.

"Good morning," said their mom. "How about some eggs and toast for breakfast."

The boys looked up at the clock that hung above the stove. It read 8:45, and they saw that they had plenty of time. "Yes" they said, "that would be good." One of the boys requested scrambled eggs and their mother asked the other if he had a preference. He said, "No". So, scrambled they were.

They knew that their mom would make any kind they said, as long as they were the same. No special orders. There were other options; French toast, soft boiled, fried eggs, but they all came out of the same pan and all hit the plate the same way. If the boys wanted fried eggs and one got broken, it was the luck of the draw and no complaints.

Poodles sat at the door at attention with his leash centered in his mouth, equal amounts hanging from either side. He needed to pant because of the excitement but, with the leash clinched between his teeth he could be heard taking quick breaths through his nose, tail wagging and fighting the urge to jump up from his sitting position, to hurry the boys.

The boys killed time, waiting for 10:00 to roll around. Their father having slept in came to the table and asked his wife for a cup of coffee, and what was for breakfast. "Scrambled eggs," his wife replied.

"I'll take 3," said the father. He didn't mention toast as he knew that would be a standard with the eggs. His wife set a mug of coffee in front of him and started whisking the eggs.

"So today you go to Rays," said the boy's father. You be sure to be respectful to him. And, tell him I was pleased to meet him.

The boys could tell that their father liked the Old man. They told their father they would be respectful and that their dad said, "He was pleased to meet him."

This brought the clock to 10:00, so the boys excused themselves and made their way out the door, hooking the leash to Poodles harness, and saying their goodbyes.

The boys walked and talked and soon found themselves on Elm Street, walked down Elm, and saw the old man's house. The boys continued on their way and passed the walk to the old man's front door, straight to the drive and walked up.

The Old mans' house was different than the house they lived in. There was no door on the side, but one in the back, with a sidewalk that came off the drive to a small step-up porch. The back screen door, unlike the aluminum one on their house was wooden, and was worn by the weather. The screen on the door was not shiny but dark and appeared to be rusted. There was a handle on the door with no knob, and a funny looking latch above the handle.

The boys knocked on the door. "Come in," said the old man. The boys opened the screen door and then the wooden door to the house and stepped inside. The screen door had a spring on it. When they let the door go it slammed against the frame and startled them. The sight and sound of the door had no effect on Poodles.

"Hello," said the old man, "you can unleash Poodles you're right on time."

"Poodles" made a dash for the old man, who bent over, patted him on the head, and rubbed him behind the ears. "Hello Poodles, how's the boy?" he said.

The house was different than the boys had imagined. Or, maybe they had not really imagined it at all. Everything caught their eye.

"Make yourself at home boys," said the old man. So, the boys removed their shoes and walked forward into the kitchen where the old man sat at the kitchen table.

"Have a seat," he said.

The boys came to the table and pulled the unfamiliar chairs out to join the old man. The chairs were steel framed and shiny, with yellow pads on the backs and on the seats.

They were soft and kind of slippery to sit on. There were knobs on the end of the chair legs so they wouldn't mark the floors. The floors were like a big sheet of plastic with a speckled pattern, and would be described as brown on tan. They were clean but had a worn look. A strip of shiny steel separated the floor in the middle, apparently there to hide the seam that joined two pieces.

The table was yellow, the same as the chairs with shiny steel tube legs that matched the chairs. There was a wide border around the table that had ridges and a slit down the middle. The table was just the right size for 4 people. One of the boys asked about the slit.

"The slit is for a leaf, said the old man. "When you put in the leaf you can seat more people at the table. It makes the table about 2 feet longer."

The counters matched the floor and had a metal strip that wrapped around the edges. The strip covered all sides of the counters.

There was a small window over the sink that looked into the back yard. It had a curtain that really didn't have any color, and pulled to the sides to let in the light and show the view of the back yard.

On the counter sat a coffee pot, not a coffee maker, a coffee pot. It was shiny steel-like and had a glass bulb on the top, and a red light on the side. The house smelled like coffee. There was a toaster that sat next to the coffee pot and each had cords that were made of some kind of brown and black cloth. A dish drainer sat to the right of the sink and had one pot, one dish, a fork, a knife and a spoon in it. Everything was tidy, but worn, and the paint on the walls was light brown but appeared faded.

"The bathroom is down that hall on the right if you need it," said the old man. "Towels are clean and there are more in the closet."

There was absolutely nothing fancy about the kitchen. It was functional and comfortable, but had a bare feel, not something you could put your finger on, but it made you feel like something was missing.

"Would you like to see the rest of the house?" asked the old man. Come-on, I'll show you around.

The boys stood up and the old man headed toward an archway that led into the living room. As soon as the old man stood up, so did Poodles. He walked alongside the old man like he had been there before.

When you had passed through the arch-way and to the left was a long wall that took you to the front door. The door was natural wood and looked very heavy, and had a mail slot, bronze colored that looked like worn gold. Next to the door on the right was a closet that would appear to be for winter coats and the like.

The wall to the left had something that looked like a dresser with doors. It was old but was shiny and well-polished. There was a cloth over the top that looked very old and had fancy edges with patterned holes that looked like flowers. You could see through the cloth to the wood of the table.

On top of the cloth sat a picture of a Soldier and another of a lady. The pictures were old and had no color, the lady had a dark hat on and what looked like a light colored suit with a white shirt that had a collar, a large pin was fastened to the lapel.

The old man said, "That's me and the bride, a long time ago."

Above the pictures on the cloth was a wall full of pictures, news-paper articles covered in glass and framed, and ribbons mounted and framed.

The boys stared at the pictures on the wall for quite a while, looking at them and wondering who they were of, and what the ribbons were for, but the old man said nothing.

"That's the davenport and you can see the TV, and then he pointed to a rocking chair, and that's my chair," he said.

The rocking chair was old and shiny, not polished shiny, but worn shiny. By the way it was introduced it was clear that it had special meaning to the old man.

The davenport had a funny plastic cover on it that fit it tight and was clear and slippery like the kitchen chairs.

"Why is there plastic on the couch?" asked one of the boys.

"I never could figure that out," said the old man, the bride had it put on when we bought it. It's been on it ever since. She had to have it, so they put it on before it was delivered." I never asked."

The Old man pointed to a door on the far end of the room. "Come on boys, he said. "I'll show you the upstairs." He opened the door, slapped his leg and Poodles ran first up the stairs.

There was no door at the top of the stairs but on the wall to the left at the end of the hall there was a window. The window had what appeared to be the same curtain as was in the kitchen, pulled the same way to the side, and allowing light to enter the hallway.

The floors through-out the house were wooden and worn. Except around the edges by the walls, where they looked new and polished, areas where there had been no traffic.

There were four doors, two on the left and two on the right. The doors on the right were open and the doors on the left were closed.

At the other end of the hall was a window that matched the one at the top of the stairs.

He started down the hall and pointed in the first room on the right. "This is mine and the bride's room," he said.

He passed the room quickly, but the boys, stopped to study it. There was a dark steel framed bed, a night stand with a lamp and a picture of the old mans' wife, and a large dresser with a mirror. It looked like the furniture down-stairs, not shiny worn but shiny polished; the large mirror set atop the dresser had a polished wooden frame. There was a dormer with a window, and the drapes matched those in the kitchen, and the windows at either end of the hall.

The next open door revealed an upstairs bathroom, functional but plain, a stand-alone sink with tubed steel legs and exposed plumbing, tee faucet handles and a toilet with raised tank and wooden flush handle. The old man said, "If you boys needed to go, at the same time, or if I am using the bathroom downstairs, you are welcome to come up here."

He turned and pointed to the one closed door, "This is Jack's room," he said but didn't open the door. He walked to the next closed door and said, "And this is Jake's room." He said no more. And continued on his path and headed down the stairs.

"Poodles" was right on his heels and as he passed back into the kitchen asked the boys, "Are you hungry or are you ready to see the garage?" They passed by the wall with all the pictures and had questions about them, but for some reason neither felt that it was the right time to ask them.

Having had their breakfast a couple of hours earlier, they weren't hungry and after seeing the house their curiosity was drawing them toward the garage.

"We can eat later," one boy said. "Let's see the garage."

The old man led the way to the garage, first him, then Poodles, and in the rears Billy and Bob. The old man held the door for "Poodles" and Billy, Billy held it for Bob and when Bob let go of the door it slammed with a loud bang.

This startled both the boys, had little effect on Poodles, but made the old man laugh. Not a chuckle, not a giggle but a laugh. This struck the boys as odd, as they had seen the old man smile many times, chuckle a few, but never heard him laugh. They liked it, and could tell that the Old Man liked it too.

There was no walk way to the garage, but you could see that at one time there had been a worn path, down to the dirt, narrow but evident.

The garage was much like the house with faded white paint and areas that showed the wood, where the paint had peeled.

There was an entry door next to the large door, for a car. The entry door seemed more worn than the rest of the garage, and had a hasp, with a pad lock. The garage seemed secured but with the house and the garage as they were, if someone had the desire to break in on the block the old man lived on, this would probably not be the target.

The Old man reached into his pocket and pulled out a small ring of keys.

There weren't many keys on the ring but all looked old and worn. He put the smallest of the keys into the padlock and gave it a twist.

The lock open and he pulled it to free the hasp and put it back on the ring mounted to the door, leaving it open.

This was a bigger event for the boys than what they had expected. The old man's motions were slow and distinct, forcing the boys to be in anticipation of his every next move, even when they knew what it was going to be.

"Poodles" on the other hand, was just glad to be along with the three of them, and hung by the old man's side.

The old man pushed on the door that dragged on the cement floor, not where you would have to push it hard but just enough to notice by the sound. Once past the rise in the floor, it swung freely and tapped the wall on the left side of the garage.

This let in just enough light to see a string on the right hand side of the door frame hanging to about eye level. The old man tugged on the string and a light over the center of the garage turned on.

The boys had never seen a device like this and their eyes followed the string form where it hung, through a series of eyes, screwed into the studs and rafters, until it got to the pull chain on the light. The boys saw this as a stroke of genius and told the Old man they had never seen anything like it.

The Old man smiled and headed for the center of the large garage door, pulled on a rope that was attached to two springs, releasing the locks on the door tracks, and allowing him to raise the door.

Another stroke of genius thought the boys, as their garage door opened and closed itself with a push of a button, a click and a buzz.

This allowed much more light to enter the garage. There were three more windows, all the same size and all with shades that were drawn, so that what was inside was not exposed.

The old man walked to each window and pulled on the shade. They rolled up quickly and spun three or four times, making a slapping sound. The boys were not sure if this was by design or just the way these shades worked. Neither asked, but every time one was released more light entered the garage and exposed a lot of stuff.

The garage was clear in the center, where there was a drain. All along the walls you could see boxes stacked, some marked and some not.

"Do you know what those are?" said the Old man pointing to one corner of the garage.

There was no reply.

"Those are saw horses," said the Old man. I would like you to pull them out and put them 5 ft. apart in the center of the garage.

He pointed at one wall.

Again, there was no reply.

"That's Ply-wood," said the old man. "I want you to take that ply-wood and center it over the saw horses. It is 4 ft. by 8 ft. That will leave you a foot and a half on either side.

There are 4 saw horses and two pieces of ply-wood. So you'll be able to make 2 tables. There are nails and 2 hammers on the work bench with a tape measure. Put 3 nails through the ply-wood and into each of the horses. When you're done come back into the house and we will have some lunch. Can you handle this or should I stay and help?"

"Yes, sir," said the boys. "We can do that."

"If you can't do it right there's no sense doing it at all," said the Old man.

"Oh, we'll do it right sir," said the boys.

The Old man turned away and broke a big smile. It tickled him how the boys had called him sir, when he gave them direction. "I'll go in and see if I can find us something to eat. Do you mind if "Poodles" comes in with me?" he asked. "Come in when the tables are finished."

"No sir, that would probably be best," Billy said. Again the old man smiled at the "Sir" and made his way with "Poodles" back into the house.

When he got to the house the Old man poured himself a cup of coffee and sat down at the kitchen table. He had only been sitting for a few minutes when Bob ran in, the door slamming behind him. "Could we have some paper and a pencil;" he asked.

"Sure," said the old man. "I should have thought of that before I asked you to work on the tables." The old man got up from his seat, went to a kitchen drawer and gave Bob, both paper and pencil. "Did you find everything else?"

"Yes we're good," said Bobby, running out the back door, it slamming behind him. Again the old man laughed. This time the laugh was only seen by "Poodles".

The boys were right at it, pulling the saw horses from the corner and putting them in the center of the garage. One of the boys said, "We might as well measure them off now." Bobby agreed and grabbed the tape measure from the work bench. They added both the 8ft plywood lengths. Bobby said, "we need to have at least 16ft to get them both in." Measured the length of the horses at 36" and used the drain as the center for width and length. Then measured 8 eight foot from the center of the drain both ways.

"I think we should make them one after the other, so if we make a mistake we catch it before we make two," said Billy. They agreed and placed one of the horses on one side of the drain and one on the other.

Bobby hooked the end of the tape on the outside of the first horse and Billy measured 5 foot to the outside of the other horse. They went from side to side and off center to make sure that it was squared off and would be perfectly in the correct positions, remembering all along that the old man had said. "If you can't do it right, there's no sense doing it at all." And more than that was their commitment to doing it right.

"If that is the case, shouldn't we measure center to center of the horses?" said Bobby. "Then we will be sure to be exactly right." He measured the width of the edge on the 2" X 4" on the horse. This is only 1 ½ inches wide, let's use the outside dimension of 5 foot and that will leave us with 1 and 1/2 foot on either end of the table. It will be easy to set to the ply-wood and we can measure, and then mark it.

"I think we should use the paper and pencil and draw it out first;" said Billy.

"You're probably right," said Bobby.

And they were glad they did. They drew the plywood and the horses in the position they described, and realized that the nails would not go into the 2 X 4's. They would leave the plan for the placement of the horses the same and add ¾ inch to the measurement of the nail line. If they did this on both ends it would put the nails right on center of the horses. Side to side they would measure in 6 inches from the edge of plywood to end of horse. And for the nail line add 1 inch. The other nail would go dead center of the plywood and the horses.

They checked and double checked themselves and decided this was the best plan.

The next step was to measure the plywood and mark it for the placement of the nails. 1 ft. 6 and ¾ in. from either end, and drew a line across. They used a steel yard stick that hung above the work bench for a straight edge.

After marking the plywood three times from both ends, they marked the center and came in 7 inches from either side, and did the same to the other sheet and started the nails in the marked locations.

They then set the plywood on top of the horses and measured 1 ft. 6 in. from the edge to the side of the 2x4 on the horse and 6 in. from either side to the ends of the horse.

Everything looked like it lined up according to plan, so Billy drove the first nail home. Bobby went to the opposing side and rechecked the measurements, in case something had moved when driving the driving the first nail. All looked good so they went around the table, one nailing and one verifying the measurements. They repeated the procedure on the second table, smiled at each other and headed in to let the old man know the task had been completed. They took the sketch and paper and pencil with them.

They hit the door running and 'Poodles" ran to meet them. The door slammed and they saw the old man sitting at the table.

At the table were 3 paper plates and 3 bowls of macaroni and cheese, three glasses of milk and 3 cookies placed at each setting on a napkin of its own. Ketchup, mustard, and relish were in the center of the table next to a platter of hot dogs.

Billy set the drawing of the tables next to the ketchup.

"Anybody interested in a cup of coffee?" said the Old man.

"We thought the milk was for us," the boys said. And all three laughed.

The old man bowed his head, "God is great God is good, we thank him for this food. By his hand we all are fed, we thank him for our daily bread. In Jesus name we pray. Amen.

They all grabbed for hot dogs and passed the mustard from left to right followed by the relish. The ketchup never left the table.

"The tables are done and set-up," said Bobby. Billy grabbed the sketch and passed it to the old man. "That is how we made them. The horses are 5 ft. apart like you asked. Maybe after we eat, you can look at them and let us know they are ok."

"Well," said the Old man. It's a quarter past one and you have to be home by 2:00 so I guess there will be time for me to do an inspection. If they are like this drawing they will be just what I was hoping for."

So the three scarfed down their lunch, ate their cookies and drank their milk. "Poodles "looked up at the old man for the last bite of his hot dog. "No dice," said the Old man.

The three jumped from the table, and the boys ran out the back, the door slamming behind them. The Old man was behind them grabbing the sketch, opening the door, patting his leg for Poodles to follow. He let the door close gently, chuckled and made his way to the garage.

When he went in the garage the first thing he noticed was the boys picking up the tools and putting them back on the work bench where they had found them.

The tables were centered in the garage with precision. The Old man slowly walked around the tables and looked at every nail and its placement, put weight on the ends of the tables to make sure all was well attached, and looked back and forth from the sketch to the tables.

The boys watched him intently, hoping he would approve of their work, and find the tables to his liking.

"You did a nice job here boys," said the old man. "Now take this sketch home and put it face down on the dining room table and let your mother know you have done so."

"You know I can't pay you but I will make it worth your while" he said.

"We're good," said the boys.

"Well, I need you to come back and do more for me;" said the old man.

"That would be great," said the boys. They started walking down the drive to make it home by 2:00.

"Thank you boys," said the old man and the boys both raised their right hand with their index finger pointing up, smiling as they walked away.

Before they got to the side walk, Billy stopped and turned around. "Sir," he said.

By this time the old man was locking up the garage, stopped and said, "What is it?"

Billy said in a very serious voice, "what should we call you?"

The boys started walking toward the old man thinking this would take a conference among friends.

"What would you like to call me?" he asked. My name is Ray, and that's ok with me.

The boys looked at each other and Bobby said, "We could but that doesn't feel right." His brother nodded in agreement.

"How about "Pops?" said the old man. "That's what they called me at work." And both boys smiled with approval.

"There we have it," said the Old man. You say Pops and I'll answer to it. You might want to tell your folks and make sure it's ok with them."

"We'll tell them," said Bobby. "But I'm sure it will be just fine with them."

"We'll see you on our walk tomorrow Pops," said Bobby, and the boys made their way home.

When they got home the boys put the sketch face down on the dining room table, and yelled to their mother, "We're home! "Pops asked us to put this face down on the dining room table. Can you take care of it?"

"Pops?" yelled back their mother.

"Yes, that's what we decided we would call him," said one of the boys. "Is that ok with you and dad."

"I have no problem with it," said the boys' mother. "And I'm sure father will be good with it also."

She made her way to the closet, pulled the shoe box from the top shelf, took it to the dining room, pulled one envelope and folded the paper sketch to the inside, and placed it neatly into the box. She took the box back to the closet and placed it on the top shelf.

Sunday morning came around and the boys after being, woken by "Poodles" showered and dressed and came to the kitchen.

Their mother and father were both at the table drinking coffee. The boys took their seats and asked their mother if they could have oat meal for breakfast.

Barb looked at Benny for approval, and he nodded with a smile, acknowledging that oatmeal would be fine for him also.

"Toast?" asked their mom.

All replied, "Yes," and she took to the cupboard to get the oatmeal and the bread and start Sunday breakfast.

"Did you get anything accomplished at Ray's yesterday?" asked the father.

"Yes," replied the boys. It was a good day. We built two tables in the garage from horses and ply-wood and nailed them."

"How did they come out?" asked their father.

Pops liked them, said we did a fine job and would like to have us come back and help him some more.

"Ray OK with you calling him Pops?" asked the father. I told you boys to be respectful."

"It was his idea," said Billy. "I asked him what he would like us to call him, and he said, "his name being Ray, it would be good with him if we wanted to call him that. But, Bobby and I didn't feel like that would be right. "He just

58

doesn't seem like a "Ray" to us. So he said; the guys at work used to call him "Pops." That seemed to fit."

"Yes," said the father, "but if you and he don't mind I think your Mother and I will continue to refer to him as Ray."

"That's good with us," said Bobby, I'm sure it will be good with him too. "Ray" seems to fit when you and mom say it."

"It sounds like you got something done, but did you have fun?" asked the mom.

"Yes" said Billy he made us lunch and showed us around his house. "Poodles" and him are getting to be really good buddies. He's got a nice house, but it isn't like ours. His upstairs is different and it's old. The whole house smells like coffee. He showed us him and his wife's room and Jack and Jakes room. And a special rocking chair that is just for him."

"His wife?" asked his mother.

"Yes," said Billy. He calls her "the bride." We didn't meet her though. We didn't meet Jack or Jake either. Pops was in the army. We saw a picture of him in his uniform. I really liked his house."

"I really liked it too," said Bobby. His back door has a spring, and the door makes a bang when it closes. For some reason, he thinks that's pretty funny."

"What did you have for lunch?" asked the mom.

"Hot dogs, macaroni and cheese, milk, and a cookie, he offered us coffee but we decided the milk would be just fine with hot dogs, and a cookie," replied Bobby. The boys looked at each other and smiled.

"And mustard and relish on the dog," said the father, with a chuckle. I think you boys have made a very good friend. That's a wonderful gift. Don't forget to give thanks for him in your prayers."

"Yes, we will," said the boys.

By that time the boys had finished their oatmeal and toast, and got themselves up from the table. They walked over to "Poodles" who was sitting at the door, at attention with his leash clenched between his teeth, panting through his nose. They clipped the leash to his harness, opened the door and both raised their right hand index finger pointed straight up to say good bye."

Their mother and father sat at the table and smiled at each other. They knew there would be more to the boys going to the Old man's house, than what the boys had realized.

Some would bring them joy and some may not, but all the same, they would be grateful that the boys would share these parts of their lives with him.

The boys were off on their walk and soon came across the old man. "Hi, Pops," Billy said, as the old man patted "Poodles" on the head and rubbed behind his ears.

"You think you'd like to come over on Wednesday and give me some more help?"

"Sure," said the boys. "Do you have something special for us to do?"

"There's a lot left to be done in the garage," he replied. "Let's make it the same time as Saturday and I will have lunch for us. See if it is ok with your parents and let me know tomorrow." All three raised their right hands and pointed their index finger to the sky and continued on with their walk. No more said.

The boys talked to their parents and defined the time they would depart, and the time they could be expected home, what they were planning on doing for the Old man, and that they would be taking "Poodles" and having lunch. All was well with them, and the plans were set.

The boys were not only responsible for what they had committed to the old man. When they got home they had plenty to do to earn their keep. The grass had to be cut, windows washed and their rooms kept clean. Their mother washed the clothes, but the boys had to put them in the corner when dirty. When their mother brought them to their room clean, they put them away in their dressers, or in the closet, and made the beds if they had been stripped.

Their father had a special way that he liked the grass cut, never the same way twice in a row. This made it easy for the boys. One would cut it on a diagonal one way, the grass would be marked and the other would do it just the opposite. Window washing, car washing, sweeping the garage, or the driveway was done by direction. When either of their parents felt like they might have too much time on their hands and be prompted to become mischievous, they were given more chores.

The boys would also help their father change the oil in the car and do minor work under his direction, to keep it in running condition. Brakes, headlights, windshield wipers, and on what seemed to be a special occasion, the changing of spark plugs.

This would always be scheduled around their baseball, basketball and walking of "Poodles". Their parents were good with this, as long as all was completed and done to their satisfaction.

The boys were becoming pretty good athletes and no longer restricted to backyard ball. Both were playing in organized leagues and the BBs' were making a name for them-selves.

Wednesday came around and the boys were just as excited as they had been the previous Saturday. They finished their breakfast, took the leash from "Poodles" mouth, attached it to his harness and started towards the old man's house.

They passed the walkway to the front door and headed down the drive, and to the back door. They knocked on the door and heard the old man yell to them to come in.

There again, the Old man sat at the table, and the boys joined him. Poodles ran to his side, the old man rubbing him behind the ears and patting him on the head.

The old man was drinking a cup of coffee and asked the boys if they would like a cup before they got started. Both declined and the Old man started in with their assignment for the day.

"Do you remember all those boxes that are in the garage?" said the Old man.

"Yes," replied the boys.

The old man started into the plan.

"I would like you to take what is in those boxes and put the contents on the tables;" he said.

"Are you having a Garage Sale?" said one of the boys.

"I'm not sure," said the old man, and continued before anything else could be said.

"I would like you to take the treasures that are in those boxes, and put them on the table. Put them in order from the front of the Garage to the back, placing the things you see of the highest value at the front of the garage and the least of value toward the rear of the garage. You will probably have to move things as you go, when you find things of more or less value.

"So you are having a garage sale." said Billy.

"No, Billy, I'm really not sure. I will have to make more decisions when your task is completed. I don't want you to put what you think will bring the best price at a Garage sale toward the front of the garage. I want you to put what you feel have the highest value, and work your way back, with no consideration to how much money it would bring if sold."

"Here are the keys," said the old man." You remember how I got in. Make sure you open the front door and the shades so you have plenty of light and can see everything clearly. If you need help you know where I am. If it's ok with you I will have Poodles stay inside with me, we will make us all lunch."

"That's fine with us," said the boys, grabbing the keys and heading out the back door, the door slamming with a bang, and the Old man chuckling.

The boys got to the door and unlocked it, released the hasp and placed the lock on the hook exactly as they had seen the old man do it. They both reached for the string to turn on the light, but Bobby got their first, smiled and pulled the string watching it slide through the eyelets. Billy went to the main door and pulled the rope releasing the latches on the rails and rolled the door up. Both went to the windows and released the shades, smiling as they got to the top and flapped as they rolled.

"I'll start on this side," said Billy.

"Ok," said Bobby, "and I will start on the other side. We can work our way back."

And they started on their review of the treasures that were in the boxes, pulling their first from either side of the garage and setting it on one of the tables. Pulling off the tape that secured them, and opening the boxes.

The first box that Billy opened was full of books. They were old and worn, and most of them had tattered pages. Obviously well used.

He said to his brother, "just a bunch of old books here. They will all go to the back table."

"Are you sure?" said Bobby "Pops" said the boxes were filled with treasures. Pull them out and we can look them over."

So his brother started to pull the books from the box one by one.

"The Old Man and The Sea," he said. "Ever hear of it?"

"No," said Billy, as he took the book from his brother's hand, and opened the front cover.

On the inside of the cover there was some writing, "To Jake, from Mom and Dad," "Happy Birthday."

This is to Jake from "Mom and Dad" he said. "We're going to have to look at the rest and decide where that should go. Pull out another one."

So his brother pulled out another book and read the title, "Robin Hood," he said, and passed it to his brother.

Again his brother opened the cover and on this one was written, "To Jack, from Mom and Dad, "Merry Christmas".

The boys continued through the books, "Captains' Courageous", "Moby Dick", "The Knights of the Round Table", "Beau Jest", and "The Grapes of Wrath" and a bunch more all gifted to either Jack or Jake, from their Mom and Dad, on a special occasion. On the very bottom of the box was a large leather bound Bible. When the cover was opened, it read. "The Johnson family Bible," and was signed, "Ray, Julie, Jack and Jake".

The boys realized this was more than sorting stuff. They looked at the number of boxes in the garage and realized this would take longer that they had first thought.

On with their task they went. Somehow all the books found themselves at the front of the garage and not toward the rear.

The box that Bobby opened had a polished wooden box in it, and had a latch on the front.

The boy opened the box and it was filled with forks, knifes, spoons and a Carving knife and Gravy bowl and ladle. They had a copper yellow tint to them, and looked very fancy but very old.

"What do you think Billy?" His brother asked.

"Forks and knives," said Billy, let's put them in the back.

"You're sure?" asked Bobby.

"No I'm not sure," said his brother. "In fact, the more I look the less sure I am about anything. I think we should get "Pops" to help us with this."

"No," said Bobby. When we are done, he will look at it. I'm getting hungry. Let's go inside and see what there is for lunch."

The boys left the garage and headed for the house. They walked this time, and in fact they walked slowly. Both of them in a separate deep thought.

They got to the door and opened it. Stepped inside and saw the table set. Three paper plates with a grilled cheese sandwich, cut in half, and 3 bowls of tomato soup, a cookie at each place on a separate napkin. Three glasses of milk, the old man set at the table with "Poodles" lying next to him.

"This going to be Ok for lunch?" asked the old man.

"Perfect," said the boys.

Billy dropped his head, "God is great God is good. We thank him for this food. In Jesus name we pray. Amen." Is that OK "Pops," he said.

"Perfect," said the Old man.

They all dug into lunch. This time there were crackers on the table and the old man took 4 out of the sleeve and passed them to his left. Crunched them up and let them fall into the soup. He pressed them down so they were totally covered and left them, picked up half his sandwich and took a bite.

The boys followed suit, four crackers, crunched, and dropped into the soup, pressed down to be covered and a bite of the grilled cheese.

"Where are Jack, Jake and the bride?" asked Billy.

"They're here," said the Old man without hesitation.

"Why haven't we seen them?" asked Bobby.

"They're in my heart," said the old man. "I'm sure in time you will see them. You may have already gotten a glimpse of them."

The boys tried the soup and crackers and as they did, thought about the walk through the house, the pictures on the wall, the Old man's chair and the walk upstairs.

They remembered him calling out the rooms, and how he called the first room on the right, "his and the brides" and how they passed the other rooms, him calling out Jake's, and Jack's without opening the doors. They thought about the books and how they addressed to the boys from their "Mom and Dad". And they thought about how they had, and still did share, books with each other as they finished them.

And they thought about the Bible, with each of the family members' signatures. And the value they had placed on the books when they first saw them, and then after they had seen the backs of the covers.

"Yes," said one of the boys, "I think we have."

"When the time is right," said the Old man I will if there is a need, tell you about them. Why don't you finish your lunch, and I will lock up the garage. Ask your parents if you can come back on Saturday so you can go back to work in the garage. I think you boys may need a couple of days to get your thoughts together about your job in the garage. I will look forward to seeing you on your walk tomorrow."

The boys finished their lunch, stacked the used paper plates on the table, and put the soup bowls, spoons and glasses in the sink. They thanked the old man for lunch, clipped the leash on "Poodles"' harness and headed for home.

The old man headed for the garage. As he entered he saw the books and the family Bible on the front of the tables. He smiled and wondered if they would hold their position, as the boys continued in prioritizing treasures.

Making Difficult Choices

When the boys got home they went at their own chores and made sure they did not fall short of the expectations of their parents. They felt themselves getting closer to the old man and could see him and his needs becoming a priority. Knowing now, that his wife and boys lived only in his heart made them feel closer still. Not because they felt like they owed anything to him, but because they felt that the old man was sharing something very dear to him, with them.

That night at dinner, the boys' father thanked them for getting their chores done and asked how the second outing to "Rays" had gone.

The excitement of the first outing had changed to quiet, deep thought about how the question could be best answered.

"It went good Dad," said one of the boys.

"Yea good," said the other.

"So what was it Ray needed done today?" asked the boys' mother.

"He had us sorting some things out in the garage," said Billy.

"Did you meet his wife?" asked the father.

"No," said one of the boys.

"Did you meet Jack or Jake?" the father asked.

"Well not really, but"...... and Billy was lost for the words he needed to explain things to his father.

"So they weren't there and Ray was all by himself?" replied the father.

"Well, no, they were there. Ray was not alone," said Bobby.

"Boys, you're not being very clear," said their Mother. "Where were Jake, Jack and their Mother?"

"They are in his heart," said the boys.

"Oh, I see," said the father. "Will you be going back?"

"Oh yes, Saturday," said the boys. In a way, that told their parents that they had important duties to tend to, and they needed to make sure and help their friend.

"If it would help you to write down how you feel, take pencil and paper and when you are done, put it face down on the dining room table," their Mother offered.

"When the time is right, if there is a need, we will do that mom," said Billy. "I think we need a couple of days to get our thoughts together." The boys picked up their dishes, put them in the sink, and followed "Poodles" up the stairs to their bed room.

Benny and Barb looked at each other over the table, and shared a half smile.

"The boys could be doing a lot of growing up in the next short while," said the Barb.

70

"I believe you are right. If there is need and the time is right, we will be there for them. I think though, these boys will be able to deal with whatever comes up," replied Benny.

The next day, the boys took their same path. "Poodles" gave them his leash and they came upon the Old man. They informed the Old man that they had talked to their parents and would be to the house on Saturday, same time. The Old man said he would have lunch for them. Everyone raised a right hand with an index finger to the sky and went on their way. A normal encounter, no change of expression from any other day they had met. "Poodles" joyfully receiving his pat on the head and rub behind the ears.

When Saturday came around the boys and "Poodles", followed the normal routine. Their mother decided on breakfast that morning, "pancakes and sausage." The syrup was on the table and they took their seats. Their father made it to the table just about the time the stack of pancakes stacked high on a platter made its way to the center of the table. Their mother had timed the sausage to be ready about the time they had all had a chance to load their plates and douse the cakes with syrup.

When the sausage was done their mother filled her cup with coffee and added to her husbands. Loaded a plate for her and asked the boys. "Are you looking forward to going to Rays today?"

The boys replied that they were but were concerned that the four hours set aside was not enough time to get the things done, visit with the old man, and have lunch.

71

"If it is ok with Ray, you boys can stay longer," said their father.

"Yes," said their mother, I will plan dinner for 5:30 and if you are not home at 2:00, I will expect you here at 5:00. I packed 3 lunches. They are in the refrigerator. Take them with you, and tell Ray that your mother and father said hello."

"Thanks," said Billy. And the boys jumped from the table, Billy grabbing the lunches, and Bobby taking the leash from "Poodles" mouth, and hooking it to his harness.

The boys were walking at a much faster pace than they had on their way home from the Old man's house on Wednesday. It may have been because what they were looking forward to finding in the boxes, seeing the Old man, or the fact that their Mom and Dad were so open to their desire to spend time with "Pops". Whatever the reason, there was pep in their steps, and smiles on their faces.

As they walked up the drive they saw that the Garage was already open, the lights were on and the Old man was standing in front of the table.

"I thought I'd give you boys a head start," said the Old man. Him not knowing that the ritual of unlocking the door, pulling the light string, opening the main door and releasing the shades was something the boys were looking forward to.

"Thanks," said the boys.

"Poodles" had made it to the old man ahead of the boys and was getting his head patted and ears rubbed. When the old man said, "What's in the bags?"

"Lunch," said the boys. "Mom made it for us." The boys unaware that one of the things the old man looked forward to, when the boys came over was making them lunch. She said to tell you she and dad said hello."

"That's very kind," said the Old man. "Be sure and thank her for me and let your parents know I said hello also."

"I'll put the bags in the refrigerator," said Billy. He dashed for the house, slung open the back door and opened the refrigerator door, as the screen door slammed behind him.

When he opened the refrigerator door, he saw a platter with 3 big hamburger patties, covered in plastic wrap, a bowl of cut fruit, and on the counter a bag of hamburger buns. There was little else in the refrigerator, but a gallon of milk, ketchup, mustard and relish.

Billy stopped and thought a minute and ran back to the garage letting the door slam.

"Mom and Dad said we could stay late," said Billy. But we have to be home by 6:30 and Mom wondered if you could make us dinner. I have to call her right away and let her know."

Bobby looked at Billy like he must have banged his head on the short trip to the kitchen and back, and hard.

"That would be wonderful," said the old man. "You run back in now and call your mother, and tell her that I will be glad to make us dinner and make sure you are home by 6:30."

Billy gave Bobby a hard look straight in the eyes, as if to say, keep your mouth shut or you'll pay.

"I'm going to tell mom we will be home at 6:30," said Bobby, and he turned toward the house ran inside, grabbed the phone from the wall and called home.

His mother answered the phone, and Billy talked fast, "Were going to be late, 6:30. "Pops" is going to make us dinner. I know we said we would be home by 5:00 but this is really important."

"Is everything Ok?" said his mother.

"Yes everything is fine." replied Billy, "Is it all right?"

"It will be fine." said his mother. "It will give me a chance to make something special for dinner for your father. You boys have a good time."

"We will," said Billy. Thanks Mom."

Billy hung up the phone, ran out the back door and heard it slam, looking up just in time to see the old man laugh.

"We're all good," said Billy, "Dinner here, home by 6:30."

"Are you sure?" said Bobby, with a tilt of the head.

"Sure as I'm standing here," said Billy.

"Well you boys get started then," said the Old man. "See that lawn chair hanging on the wall?"

"Yes," said one of the boys.

"If you would pull it down and set it up by the back door on the grass, "Poodle's and I will sit in the back yard. We can have our lunch out here too."

"Sure," said Billy. And pulled the chair down and put it in by the door as directed.

The Old man made his way to the chair, "Poodles" by his side, and the boys went to work on the boxes.

Billy on one side and Bobby on the other each pulled down their first box.

The box Billy pulled down was full of toys, trucks, dozers and tractors, much like the ones the boys had when they were younger, but these were made of steel and had rust and looked well worn.

They took the toys from the box and moved them toward the back of the tables.

Bobbie's box had a bunch of dog stuff. Two bowls, one marked food and the other water, a leash, 4 or 5 balls, a tooth worn stick, a blanket and collar. The collar had a name plate riveted to it. The plate had the name **"RUSTY"** in bold letters pressed into the steel.

Bobbie walked to the front door of the garage and said, "Hey Pops." Did you used to have a dog named "Rusty?"

"No, said the Old man. "But my boys did. Let me see what you got there".

So Billy ran it out to the old man, with Bobby on his heels.

75

Billy handed it to the old man, and "Poodles" jumped up and as the old man held it, sniffed it and wagged his tail.

"Humph," said the old man. "I haven't seen this in a long time."

"Poodles" sniffed and sniffed, and wagged his tail and went down on his haunches. He yipped at the collar and made one heck of a fuss.

"Poodles" seems to like it," said the old man. Think we should put it on him and see if he likes to wear it?"

"Well," said Billy, "Poodles has never had a collar and he's black and white. There's nothing rusty about him."

"Yea," said Bobby but he really seems to like it, and it can't hurt to put it on him. Let's try it, we can always take it off if it doesn't fit."

So the boys took the collar from the Old man and put it on "Poodles". No sooner did they get it on him than the dog laid next to the old man with his head resting on his front paws, stopped wagging his tail and relaxed.

"Fits him just right," said Billy, and the boys and the Old man looked at "Poodles" in the old collar and smiled. The boys headed back to the Garage and the old man patted "Poodles" on the head.

Time was passing. The boys kept sorting, and placing treasures on the table. They had come to find that their first look, and where they first thought the article should be placed, was not always a fit. But continue they did, finding baseball gloves with the names Jake and Jack written in magic marker on them, old baseball bats and footballs, jerseys and caps, fine China, and shoes, comic books and crochet needles, with scans of yarn.

"You boys getting hungry," asked the old man. "I'm going inside to get the lunch your mom made us. If you want anything to drink you can fill a glass when you go in to wash your hands."

While the Old man went and got the sack lunches, the boys headed for the bathroom to wash-up. They asked the old man if he wanted them to bring him something to drink.

"Ice water for me," said the old man. "There's ice in the trays in the freezer."

Billy went outside with the Old man and Bobby went to the cupboard and got three tumblers out to fill with ice and water. He opened the refrigerator and saw Freezer written across the face of a door that swung down, made of aluminum. He pulled on the top of the door and it creaked as it opened. It pulled hard as though there was something in the way.

When he got it all the way open, he could see what was interfering with the door. Ice was built up all around the inside of the freezer. It was probably an inch thick and white like hardened packed snow.

On top of the ice were two aluminum ice cube trays with a funny looking handle on the top. Bobby had never seen this ice condition in the freezer at home and when he pulled the trays out they were stuck to the ice and he really had to tug on them.

"You need help with that water?" asked the old man.

"I'm not sure," said Bobby, "Maybe."

The old man got up from his chair and Poodles followed him into the house. Billy came in to see how this had become an unmanageable chore for his brother.

"I see you found the ice," said the old man, and the glasses."

"Yes," said Billy. "But the freezer is packed with ice all the way around and I had to tug on these handles to get the trays unstuck."

The old man smiled. "That freezer hasn't been defrosted for a long time," he said. "Turn the water on in the sink and run it over the top of the trays, let it set a minute and you can pull up on the handle. "That will break the ice loose and you can put it into the glasses."

"Our ice cube trays are plastic," said Billy, "and they don't have any handles like this. You just twist them and the ice falls right out. Our freezer doesn't freeze up like that either."

"I'm sure not," said the old man. "Your folks have a frostless refrigerator. This one is probably as old as your father. Every so often you have to turn it off and let the ice in the freezer section, melt enough so you can chip it out. They quit making those kinds of trays when the plastic ones came out, but in their day they were probably as popular as the pop-up toaster when it came out."

The old man took the tray and pulled up on the handle breaking the ice loose. He pulled out the separator and placed it in the sink. Put 4 cubes a piece in the tumblers and

78

filled them with water. All and all things worked out pretty well as Billy would have had a heck of a time carrying three full glasses to the back yard, and he got a lesson in the past practice of making ice cubes. Defrosting freezers and how his grandmother would have handled getting the three of them water had she been given the task.

They found their seats in the back yard, the old man in the lawn chair and the boys sitting in the grass either side of the dog.

The old man opened his bag first.

"Let's see what your mother put together for us for lunch," he said.

He reached into the bag and pulled out a sandwich. The boys did the same and all removed the wrappings at the same time.

The old man took a bite and said, "Bologna and cheese with mayonnaise and sliced tomato. How did your mother know this was my favorite kind of sandwich?"

"She must have just been lucky," said Billy.

The old man bowed his head and closed his eyes and said, "God is great. God is good. We thank him for this food. In Jesus name we pray. Amen," through the bite of sandwich in his mouth.

"I'd say we are all pretty lucky," said the old man, as he pulled an apple and chips from the bag, still chewing his bite of sandwich. "This is a very good lunch. Be sure and thank your mother for me when you get home."

79

About that time, a man the boys had never seen came into the back yard from the drive way. He was about the same age as their father and had on blue jeans with a blue work shirt. The shirt had a name tag with red letters, and the name on it was "Charlie." His hands were dirty and looked like he had been working on something greasy. He had a hat on, and there was a smudge of grease on his cheek.

"How you doing "Pops?" he asked the old man.

"Good, Charlie," the old man replied. "Come over here and meet the BBs. Billy and Bobby."

"So these are the bookends you were telling me about," said Charlie. "How do you know which is Billy and which is Bobby?"

"Well," said the old man, "you have to ask their mother."

The boys laughed. First because the old man told Charlie he'd have to ask their mother for proper identification, and also because of all the things they had been referred to as twins, this was the first anyone had called them bookends.

"Boys," said the old man. "Say hello to Charlie, he's dirty and greasy and I'm pretty sure his feet stink. But he'd never do anything, to harm anyone."

"Hi Charlie," said the boys.

"And this must be "Poodles," said Charlie, named from a pile of.........

Before he could get another word out, the old man interrupted and said, "Yes Charlie this is "Poodles."

I see the boys are hard at it "Pops," said Charlie.

"Yes they are," said the old man, "and doing a fine job."

"You ok?" Charlie asked the old man.

"Just fine," the old man replied.

"You sure?" said Charlie with a hand on the old man's shoulder.

"Sure as I'm sitting here," said the Old man.

Charlie turned and started walking away, raised his right hand index finger to the sky and said, "Nice meeting you boys, enjoy your time with "Pops".

"Nice meeting you too," said the boys. "We always enjoy our time with "Pops."

The old man and the boys finished their lunch and crumpled up the bags. Taking the last bite of the apple the old man threw the core to the back fence. "Something will be glad to eat that," he said.

The boys took the last bite of their apples and threw the cores to the fence. Went back into the garage and got back to pulling treasures from boxes.

The job that was so daunting became pleasurable. The placement of the treasures was not as important as the examination, as they saw the tables filling and the boxes emptying.

It was about 4:00 when the old man got up from his chair and headed into the house. "Poodles" followed him in and he made his way to the living room. He sat and rocked and told, Poodles what a good dog he was, and that his boys and Rusty would be glad to see he had taken ownership of the collar.

About half an hour had passed and the old man fell asleep in the rocker. Poodles laid next to him as the Old man quietly sighed in his sleep.

The house was just dark enough so when you came into the living room, you either had to let your eyes adjust, or turn on the light, mounted to the ceiling in the center of the room. It was a comfortable room for the old man and he would use it for his nap on a regular basis. On this occasion he gladly shared the solitude with "Poodles."

Many times as he slept, he would dream of his wife and boys, or of his service in the Army. Naps were a pleasure to the Old man, and he looked forward to what he would see in his dreams. They had become an escape from loneliness and he considered them a gift.

Shortly after 5:00, the boys looked at each other and said, "Let's take a break and see what "Pops" is up to.

The boys ran to the house, slung open the door and as they entered the kitchen. It slammed with a mighty crack, expecting to see "Pops" sitting at the kitchen table drinking a cup of coffee. "Poodles" broke through the archway at a dead run, as the old man called from the living room. "I'm out here resting my eyes."

The boys walked into the living room and saw "Pops" in his chair.

"Turn on the light, Billy," he said.

Billy flipped the switch and the light came on.

The boys were left standing in front of the wall with all the Pictures, ribbons, and News Paper articles.

"What are all these?" asked Billy.

"Pictures and the like, of things I look back on with fond memories," said the Old man.

"Who's this?" asked one of the boys, and he pointed to one of the pictures on the far left side of the collection.

"That's Jake," said the old man. "He's about 3 in that picture, and this one over here is Jack at the same age."

"They were twins like Bobby and I." said Billy. His voice showed excitement, expecting to hear the old man confirm the statement."

"No," the old man replied. "They were born a year apart. But they were a bit like you and your brother. They'd let the door slam when they came in or left the house. Their mother never could break them of that."

"We're sorry, said the boys. "We thought that was just the way the door worked."

"Nothing to be sorry about," said the old man. "I always figured the door should work that way too. Never could understand why it bothered the bride," and he laughed.

The way the boys had heard him laugh the first time they had let the door slam, "I'm not really sure it bothered her at all. I think sometimes she just liked to bark."

Then Bobby pointed to a picture of two boys and a dog. "This must be Rusty," he said.

"Yes, that's Rusty," said the old man. He looked down at "Poodles and patted him on the head, reading the tag that was riveted to his collar. "Rusty was an "Irish Setter." The boys loved him, and he loved the boys, they shared him with me."

"Like "Poodles", said Billy.

"I really appreciate you boys sharing "Poodles" with me," said the old man.

"Are you kidding "Pops"? Said one of the boys, with an excited voice, "Poodles" loves you!"

"And I love him," said the Old man, and he reached down with both hands looked "Poodles" in the eye and rubbed behind his ears.

"It's getting late," said the old man. "I have some burger in the fridge, how about we go out and fry one up. Have some fruit too. We'll have that for dinner. If you open the end door on the buffet, you'll find a photo album. You can bring it into the kitchen and look at it while I make the burgers."

One of the boys opened the end door and pulled out the album. The old man went into the kitchen and took an old Iron skillet from the cupboard.

As he placed the skillet on the burner he reached the back of the stove and grabbed a box of stick matches. He turned the knob on the stove to the right, lit the match with one hand on his thumb nail and "pop" the flame jumped up on the stove.

To the old man, this was just lighting the stove, but to the boys, it was about as close to magic as anything they had ever seen.

"How did you light that match?" said Bobby?

"Pretty well, I think," said the old man.

"But you just flicked it with your thumb and it lit," said Billy.

"Strike anywhere matches," the old man replied." I've been doing it this way for as long as I can remember."

"Can you teach me?" asked Bobby.

"Is there something you want to light on fire?" replied the old man. "If so I can. But you know better than to play with fire, here each of you take a match."

So the old man pulled one from the box himself and wrapped his fingers around it, the head of the match just above the center fold in his index finger. He put his thumb nail on the white of the match and quickly pulled his nail over the match head. When it lit he released the match from his index finger and held the match with his second finger and moved the match through his hand, so he was only holding the unlit end.

"Now you try it," said the old man.

85

So the boys did. Over and over and over, but could not get it to light.

"It's kind of like whistling through your teeth. You have to practice and keep trying till you get a tweet and work on it from there. Put the matches back in the box and we can try it again another time."

"Will you show us how to whistle through our teeth?" said one of the boys.

"Another time, but now I am making us burgers," he replied.

By this time the skillet was hot, and he took the burgers and dropped them one at a time into the pan.

The burgers "sizzled" and as they cooked he reached into the cupboard, pulled out three paper plates, and three bowls.

He took the burger buns from the counter and set them on the table.

These were some big buns and the patties he put in the pan were huge. Next he went to the fridge and grabbed the ketchup, mustard and relish, and set them on the table. Then he returned for the mixed fruit.

"Will burgers and fruit be enough for your dinner?" he asked.

"Yes," said the boys, "Those are some big burgers."

"I think I can find some cookies for dessert, he said. He reached up into a different cupboard pulled out some windmill cookies, and three glasses. He went back to the stove and flipped the burgers, moving right back to the refrigerator for the milk, and setting it on the table.

"Onion," he asked?

"None for us," replied the boys.

The boys were looking through the photo album. There were all kinds of pictures of the old man and his family. He looked much younger in the pictures. But there weren't any pictures of any of the family that showed any of them as older.

Birthdays, baseball games, basketball games, family camping and in a lot of them "Rusty." They all had big grins and seemed to be having fun, in every picture.

The Old man put the burgers on the table. "Dress them up," he said.

The boys waited for the old man to sit down. Bobby picked up the milk and filled all three glasses. The Old man took a fork and stabbed one of the burgers, put it on the bottom bun and pulled the fork. He reached for the ketchup and added a healthy dose.

Bobby closed his eyes and bowed his head. "God is great. God is good. We thank him for this food. In Jesus name we pray, Amen."

The boys stabbed their burgers, put them on the buns and took turns with the ketchup. Putting the same amount on theirs as did the old man.

Then the old man grabbed the mustard, opened the jar and took a knife dipping it in the jar. He took the knife out and spread the top bun with a light coating.

Just before laying the top of the bun on the burger, he picked up the sweet relish, dipped a spoon in and filled it, dropping the relish on top of the ketchup, dead on center of the burger. The boys dressed their burgers exactly the same way. And all three bit into them at the same time.

"This is the best burger I have ever had," said Billy, with a full mouth.

"Me too," said Bobby.

The old man filled his bowl with fruit and filled the bowls of the boys while they enjoyed the dinner he had made for them.

The three ate their fruit and each had a windmill cookie, finished their milk, and put the bowls and dishes in the sink.

"Would you like me to wash these?" asked Billy.

"No," said the old man. It will give me something to do after you leave. I'll close up the garage and make sure the shades are pulled. You boys should be on your way. It's after 6:00. I'm sure your parents would like some time with you today too."

"Ok," said the boys. Hooking the leash to Poodles and running out the back door, letting it slam as they went toward the drive.

The boys ran most all the way home, came into the house slipped off their shoes and unleashed "Poodles".

"Hi Mom, Hi Dad," yelled the boys.

"Hello boys," called back their mom. "Did you have a nice time at Rays?

"Oh, yea," said Billy. "Pops" said to thank you for the lunch. How did you know his favorite sandwich was bologna and cheese with a slice of tomato and mayonnaise?"

"Just lucky I guess," said the boy's mother.

"That's what we thought too," said the boys.

"How did it happen that Ray had you stay for supper?" She asked.

"Yea," how did that happen, asked Bobby?

"Well," said Billy. "When we got there and told Pops you had made us lunch, I ran into the house to put the bags in the refrigerator."

When I put the bags in, I saw that he had made up burger patties for us for lunch. I know he really liked the lunch you packed. He even shared the apple core with whatever lives out by the fence.

Anyway when I saw the burgers and then saw the buns on the counter and a bowl of fruit all cut up sitting next to the burgers, I knew he had planned for us to eat with him. So I ran back out and told him that we could stay late if he could feed us dinner, but we had to home by 6:30. He said we could stay and that it would be perfect if we stayed for dinner. I figured it would be, and told him I had to call you right away and let you know it was ok. I really like him mom and I didn't want him to feel bad and I don't think he has a lot of money and it wouldn't have been right to have them go to waste."

"Probably he and Charlie would have had the burgers," said Bobby.

"Who is Charlie?" asked their mother.

"We hadn't met Charlie yet, Bobby," said his brother.

"That's right," said Bobby.

"Who is Charlie?" Their mother asked again.

"Oh he's this dirty greasy friend of Pops," said Bobby. "Pops" isn't sure but he thinks his feet stink. He sure wouldn't do anything to hurt anyone."

"How do you know he wouldn't hurt anyone?" asked their mother.

"Pops said he wouldn't," replied one of the boys. He called us book ends, said we were getting a lot done, and asked Pops twice if he was doing ok.

"What did "Pops" I mean "Ray" say," asked his mother.

"He said he was just fine; replied one of the boys, and when Charlie touched him on the shoulder and asked him if he was sure, he said sure as I am sitting here". Then Charlie left and told us to enjoy our time with "Pops". We said, "We always did" and he left.

The conversation was drawing Barbs interest, and she asked Benny to come in from the other room.

"The boys had a very interesting day today, "she said to her husband. "Met a friend of Ray's named Charlie, and had burgers for dinner. I guess Ray really enjoyed the Bologna sandwiches I made."

"He sure did;" said Billy. "Come here "Poodles" and show dad your new collar."

"Poodles" ran up and sat next to Billy. The boys' Dad leaned over and patted the dog's head and said, "Rusty", It's a nice collar but are you sure you want to change "Poodles" name? He is pretty used to it and may not be able to adjust to the change."

"Oh," replied Bobby. "We aren't going to change his name, that's the collar that Jack and Jakes dog had."

"His name was "Rusty". We found it in one of the boxes in the garage and showed it to "Pops", he thought "Poodles" might like it so we tried it on him, and sure enough "Pops" was right. It seems to fit him just fine. "Rusty" was an "Irish Setter" and the boys shared him with "Pops" kind of like we share "Poodles" with him," said one of the boys. "Pops" thanked us for sharing "Poodles" with him, and we told him it was no problem cause "Poodles" loves him, and he said that he loved "Poodles" too."

"Well," said their father, "What other kind of treasures are you finding in the garage?"

"Books and toys and china," said the boys. "All kind of things dog toys and bowls.

Jake and Jack played a lot of sports. There are baseball gloves and bats, footballs, and shoes. And a wooden box with knives and forks that are really old, and kind of yellow. We're just about done in the garage, most everything is on the tables. We haven't done very well at putting them in the order of value. It's really hard. Not money value but true value. We just pull treasures from the boxes and put them on the tables"

"Treasures," their father said. Is "Ray" having a Garage sale?"

"I don't think so Dad; said the Bobby. We asked him the same thing and he said he would have to decide what the right thing was to do. We're just pulling them from the boxes looking them over real close and deciding what the value is."

"What else did you do?" asked the boys' mother.

"When we came in before dinner," said Billy with excitement in his voice. "Pops" was in the living room sitting in his chair with "Poodles." He called us to come in there, and we looked at pictures of him, his wife, and Jake and Jack on the wall. "Rusty" was in some of the pictures too. Rusty was really pretty. Have you ever seen an "Irish Setter"? That's when "Pops" told us about how his boys used to share "Rusty" with him and thanked us for sharing "Poodles" and said that he loved "Poodles". He told us to get a photo album from the buffet that has a picture of him and his wife on it, under the pictures on the wall. So we did and we took it out and looked at it while "Pops" made us burgers."

"Sounds like quite a day, said Benny. "And yes I have seen an "Irish Setter". They are beautiful dogs."

The boys' Dad reached down and patted "Poodles" on the head. "And of course "Poodles is a beautiful dog too," he said."

"Yea," said Bobby, "Runts" are beautiful dogs."

"When will you be going back," asked their mother.

"Probably Wednesday, we'll ask "Pops" when we see him on our walk tomorrow," replied Bobby.

The boys woke for their day and got their chores out of the way.

They went for their walk and soon saw "Pops" approaching. Before the boys could get the words out, the Old man said, "Going to see you boys on Wednesday?"

The boys said, "Yes, we will be there the same time. Should we ask mom to make lunch?"

 "If you like," said the old man. As he rubbed Poodles ears, "see if you can stay till 5:00."

"Will do," said the boys, and off they all went. Their right hand in the air index finger pointing up, the traditional sign of departure.

When the boys got home, they told their mother they would be at the Old mans on Wednesday and that they would be staying until 5:00. Ask her if she would pack three lunches and would plan on dinner at home. She asked if the same thing would be good as she had made before, and the boys said, "That's "Pops" favorite and it would be perfect."

On Tuesday, the boys had a baseball game and it was a doozy. They both had hits and made good plays in the field, and were on their game. The team was glad to have their bats and their gloves and they were ahead by 2 runs in the 2nd, when it started to rain.

It rained and it rained. The boys waited in the dugouts for it to stop but it just wasn't going to happen. The umpire called the game and scheduled a make-up for the next day, Wednesday.

The boys went to their coach and told him that they were expected to help their friend and would not be able to be able to play in the make-up game.

The boys were a critical part of the team and with them; the team would have a very good chance of winning and without them near certainty of defeat. The coach was going to do what was necessary to have them there.

The coach asked the boys. "Is there anything you can do to make different plans?"

Billy replied, "This is really important and we would rather miss the game than disappoint our friend."

"This must be some friend," said the coach.

"Oh yes," said the boys, "the best ever." We see each other almost every day and mom is making us lunch to take to his house and the plans are set."

"And there is nothing you can do to make a change in these plans?" replied the coach. "Any chance I can talk to this friend?"

"I don't know," said Billy, "what would you want to talk to him about?"

"About you playing ball tomorrow," replied the coach, trying not to show his frustration, with the boy's priorities.

Billy held up his right and index finger to the sky, turned and took 3 steps away from the coach. His brother followed and the boys had a conference.

When they were done talking it over they turned back to the coach and said, "We're going to have to ask our parents if it's ok."

The coach rolled his eyes and said, "Who would have figured?"

"How about I give you boys a ride home," he said. "I'll talk to your parents and if it's ok with them we can go over to your friend's house and ask him if it's ok to change your plans with him and play in tomorrows' game."

Bobby raised his right hand, turned around and took 3 steps back. His brother followed. They talked to each other for a couple of minutes, and turned back to the coach.

"You know where we live coach? It takes us about 15 minutes to get there. We will run so it will probably be 10," said Billy. "Mom says we can't ride home with anybody rain or shine unless she or dad knows about it. If you want to drive over to our house we will hustle home and you can talk to our mom."

95

"Boys," said the coach. "I'm your coach. I'm sure it would be OK if you rode with me to your house."

"That may be," said the boys. "And if you want to ask our mom if it is ok if you give us a ride home you can do that. But this time we walk."

"Good grief," said the coach. "OK, I will meet you at your house in 10 min. You boys sprint. Consider it part of your practice. If anyone asks why you're running so fast, you tell them your coach said you had to run fast all the way home as part of your practice."

The boys took off like a flash and the coach walked to his car shaking his head and smiling. He knew the boys were doing the right thing, and respected them for it. He thought back on when he was a boy and wondered if he would have had the same respect for his parents' wishes as the boys had for theirs.

As time would have it, the boys saw the coach's car turning the corner on their street, about the same time they were making it to the drive. They smiled at each other and slapped high fived, celebrating making the drive before the coach. The coach saw this and chuckled.

The coach got out of the car and walked up the drive to the side door of the house. When they opened the door, they invited the coach in and yelled for their mother. "Poodles" was waiting at the door and jumped all over the boys. When the boys didn't take their dog with them, he acted like it had been a lifetime, when they met up.

The boys' mother walked into the kitchen, asked the three of them if everything was all right and when she was assured all was well, offered the coach a seat and a cup of coffee.

The coach accepted and she poured a cup, "do you like anything it," she asked.

"Black is fine," said the coach. He took a sip of the coffee and thanked the boys' mother.

"The reason I am here, he said. Is to see if it is ok if the boys.... NO that is not the reason I am here."

He had learned that with this family that following protocol was the path to success.

"Boys," he said. Do you have something to ask your mother?"

The boys' mother smiled, looked away from the coach, and at her sons.

"Our game got rained out today," said Billy. And it's rescheduled for tomorrow. The coach thinks it's best if we play, but we have plans to go over and see "Pops". When we told the Coach that we wouldn't be able to play because we had already made plans, he wanted to go and talk to "Pops" and see if something else could be worked out. Bobby and I talked about it, and told him that we would have to ask you if it is ok for him to talk to "Pops". So, he made us run home as part of the practice and drove over here to see if it would be OK."

"Well, how do you think "Ray" would feel about it?" asked their mother. "He's a good friend to you boys and you made a commitment to him."

97

"That's the way we saw it mom," said one of the boys. "But coach said he wanted to talk to "Pops" to see if there was a way for us to play tomorrow."

As the coach listened to the conversation, he was seeing that the ballgame was more important to him than it was to anyone else. That didn't have any effect on how he felt about things, but it was becoming painfully apparent that if he didn't step up to the plate and get his swings in, they would be playing two men short tomorrow.

"What the boys say is absolutely correct," said the coach, measuring every word. The facts of the matter being, that if these boys don't play tomorrow, we aren't going to get into the championships and I sure wouldn't want to have them miss out on that."

The words no sooner leaving his lips knowing that he knew he had measured them wrong.

"Yes," said their mother. "I am sure that they would be very disappointed if they didn't play in the championships." But I think we were talking about them making a commitment to their friend and how their friend would feel. Not a doubt in my mind these two boys would be able to deal with not playing in the championships. Do you agree boys?"

"Sure do mom; that's why we told coach we had to ask you if he could talk to "Pops".

"Well, I don't guess it would do any harm, for him to talk to Ray," replied their mother, but on one condition."

"What's that?" asked the coach eagerly.

"Well actually I am talking to the boys, coach," said their mother. "This decision is between you and "Pops". And if you feel in any way that you will damage the trust you have with him, or if he is anyway uncomfortable with this, you hold fast to your plans, with him. This is a decision you and your friend have to make, and he should be your first consideration."

By this time the coach had begun wondering if even he cared about the championships. But if there was one thing you could clearly see about the coach, he was determined, and willing to change course if it helped him to his destination.

"Oh," said the coach. Would it be ok if the boys rode over to their friends' house with me, in my car?"

"Are you boys taking Poodles?" asked their Mother.

"Yes," said the boys, "Poodles" and "Pops" both would be disappointed if we didn't bring him."

"Are you OK with a dog going in your car Coach?" their mother asked.

At this point, the coach would have agreed to let the dog drive.

"Just fine with me," said the coach, I'll bring the boys and "Poodles" home when we are done talking to their friend."

"You all have a good time," said the boys' mother. "And tell Ray I said hello."

The boys gathered "Poodles" leash and the four of them scooted out the door, the coach leading the pack.

Being "Pops" only lived three blocks away the ride in the car was short.

The coach pulled into the drive and all jumped out, Poodles pulling on the leash to get to the old man. They walked around the back and Billy banged on the wooden door. The main door was open, and they heard a "Who's here," from inside the house.

It's Bob and Billy," the boys called back.

"Our coach is with us. Can he come in?" asked one of the boys.

"Is "Poodles" with you?" asked the Old man?

"Yes," replied Bobby, through the screen door.

"Well then, I guess you can all come in," replied the old man.

Bobby opened the door, unleashed "Poodles" and he made a dash for the living room. The boys and the coach followed.

When they entered the dimly lit room they could see the old man sitting in his chair, "flip that switch Bobby," said the old man.

So Bobby flipped the switch. As their eyes were adjusting to the dim light and they could see "Poodles" and the old man making up for lost time.

"Have a seat on the davenport," he said.

The coach moved toward the couch and the boys studied the wall for just a minute and then made their way to the couch. The old man smiled at the fact that the boys wanted to get another look at his treasures on the wall and from his rocking chair asked the boys what had brought them to his house on a Tuesday.

The coach spoke up and said, "I guess it's …………"

And before he could finish the sentence the old man said, "Actually sir I was asking the boys. Would you like to introduce me to your coach boys?"

"Yes sir," said Bobby, "Coach this is "Pops." "Pops" this is coach. We had him come to our house to ask our mom if it was ok if he came over and talk to ask about something."

"And what did your mother say?" asked the old man.

She said, she could find nothing wrong with having the coach come over to talk to ask you something, but the decision had to be between, you and us.

And if we feel in any way that it will damage the trust you have with us, or if you is anyway uncomfortable with this, to hold fast to our plans with you.

This being a decision to be made by us and our friend, and you and our commitment to you should be our first consideration.

"And how do you boys feel about what your mother said?" replied the old man.

"We were plenty good with it "Pops," said the boys. "Actually we had already made up our minds, but the

101

coach wanted to come and see if we could make some other arrangements."

The coach was feeling like he was standing out in left field and there was a meeting at home plate.

"So, Coach, said the old man. Sounds like you have something pretty important on your mind. I don't know how I come into the play, but throw me the ball and I'll see if I can catch it."

"Well, said the coach. "I coach the boys in baseball, and we had a game today."

"Humph," said the old man. "It rained pretty hard today. How'd you get a game in?"

"Well that's the thing sir," said the coach.

"Oh you don't have to call me sir," said the old man. The boys call me "Pops" if you feel comfortable with that you're welcome to do the same, if not you can call me "Ray" that's what their folks call me."

"Ok," said the coach, anxious to get back to the point.

"Well?" asked the old man.

"Well what," said the coach.

"Well are you going to call me "Pops" or are you going to call me "Ray"? asked the old man.

The old man smiled, and the boys giggled. The coach wondered if he was being played with.

The boys and the old man, and probably "Poodles" knew.

"It's like this, "Pops"," said the coach.

"Oh you decided on "Pops"," said the old man. "I was hoping you would decide to call me "Pops". The boys call me "Pops" you know."

"As I was saying," said the coach. "We had a game today, and weren't able to get the whole thing in because of the rain."

"My boys played ball," said the old man. "That's them on the wall there."

'"Yes, that's nice," said the coach as he glanced at the wall and looked up at "Pops".

Then out of nowhere, the coach jumped up from the couch and looked at the wall.

"Jake and Jack were my boys," said the old man.

"You're Jake and Jacks Johnsons father," said the coach.

"Yes, I am," said the old man.

The coach walked over to a team picture hanging on the wall.

The coach took his right hand and pointed to one of the players on the picture. "Do you remember me?" he asked. "That's me standing next to Jack. Man those kids were some good ball players."

"Nate Crowley," said the old man. "Jake at third, Jack at Short, and you at second, between the 3, there were a lot of double plays turned."

"Yes sir," said the coach. "I've changed my mind; I would like to call you "Sir".

"Thank you," said the old man. "What do you need Nate?"

"It's like this Sir," the coach replied. "We got rained out today and the game is rescheduled for tomorrow. I need the boys to play, or we won't have a chance against the team we are playing.

They told me that they had plans with their friend tomorrow and they would not be able to play. So I told them that I would like to meet their friend and see if something could be worked out. They're the backbone of the team. Kind of like Jack and Jake were."

"First off, I can't begin to tell you how nice it is to see you Nate. Second off if you need the boys to play tomorrow I would be glad to adjust my schedule. But there are two conditions, first and for most when we are done here, I would like the boys to take you to the garage. You will find all of Jake and Jack's gear out there. I would like the three of you to decide who on your team would benefit the most from the gear and give it to them. Will you do that for me?"

"Nate and the boys said they would. All replied at the same time."

"What is the other condition?" asked Bobby.

"The other condition is that your coach picks me up before your game and let me sit on the bench with the team, and watch you play. If it is allowed, I would like to have "Poodles" there with me."

"I'll pick you up at 12:30," said Nate. "If it's OK with you the boys and I will go to the garage and get the gear now."

The old man pulled the keys out of his pocket and handed them to Billy. "The boys know how to get in the garage and make sure you have enough light. Bobby, you can leave the key hanging in the lock when you are done. I will come out and lock it up."

"Don't you want to come out," asked Bobby?

"No," said the old man. "I've been out there every day this week. I've seen what I needed to see. Be sure and bring "Poodles" to the game with you. I don't want him to miss any of the action."

As they were walking out, Nate turned to the old man and said, "I'm sorry for your loss, Sir."

The old man smiled and said, "Thank you."

The boys and the coach loaded up the car with all the baseball gear that was on the table. Leaving no remnant, "Poodles" jumped into the car with the boys and Nate following. Nate drove the boys home and said, "Be to the field at one o'clock."

The boys and "Poodles" entered the house, their father sitting at the table and their mother over the stove. They heard the coach honk his horn as he pulled from the drive and drove off.

"What have you and Ray decided on?" asked their mother.

"We're going to play," said the boys.

"Really," said their mother, surprised at the response having expected to hear just the opposite.

"What are we talking about here?" asked their father.

"Our game got rained out today," said Billy, and got re-scheduled for tomorrow. We were going to go to "Pops" house tomorrow and told the coach we wouldn't be there. He took us over to see "Pops" and they talked and "Pops" and "Poodles" are going to the game to watch. They're going to sit on the bench with the team. Coach used to play ball with Jack and Jake, his picture was on the wall standing next to Jack in one of the team pictures. He played second, Jack played short, and Jake played third. Between the three of them they turned a lot of double plays. Coach said, he would like to call "Pops" "Sir", and "Pops" thanked him. Then he told "Pops" he was sorry for his loss, and "Pops" thanked him again."

"We went out in the garage and got all Jake and Jacks' baseball gear together and put it in the coaches' car. "Pops" didn't come out though. He said he had been out there every night for the last week and had seen what he needed to see. Coach is going to give the equipment to the boys on the team that can use it."

"That's very kind of "Pops," said their father.

"Yea," said the boys. Coaches' name is "Nate". "Pops" knew him and everything."

"That's nice," said the boys' mother. "And how nice "Ray" and "Poodles" can sit on the bench with the team and watch the game."

The boys' mother set the table and put a big bowl of goulash in the center of the table. This was one of the boys and their dads' favorites. Their mom put kidney beans in the goulash, something her mother had done and everyone liked it that way. Though had the boys had their way, the beans would not have been in the mix.

"God is great. God is good. We thank him for this food. By his hand we all are fed, we thank him for our daily bread. In Jesus name we pray, Amen. Prayed Billy, with his head bowed and his eyes closed.

The family started into the goulash and enjoyed every bite. When the boys finished up they took "Poodles upstairs with them and talked awhile. Their father came into the room and asked if they had anything to tell him?

They thought for a minute and said, "No". Kneeling by the side of the bed, waited for their father to leave the room and said their prayers.

The night went fast and boys rose early. It was a bright and sunny day and they got around quickly. They went to the kitchen with "Poodles" and went outside to get at their chores.

Their mother was not in the kitchen when they came down, but shortly after called out the window to see what the boys would like for breakfast.

"Eggs are good, mom. You decide what kind," said Billy.

"I'm going with chicken eggs," called out their mom.

The boys laughed and kept at their chores. When their mother had finished making breakfast she called them in.

The boys sat and ate and their mother sat with them. She loved her boys and was very proud of them. She knew they were not perfect, because their father kept lists. But had she had two boys, or five boys and girls, she would love them with all her heart and show them every day.

The morning went fast, and soon it was time to get ready to go play ball. They went to their room and saw that their mother had dried the uniforms from yesterdays' rain and had them laid out on the bed for the boys to put on.

The boys put on the uniforms and got their gloves and headed down the stairs. Poodles for some reason knew he would be invited and was turning in circles by the back door.

It was a quarter to 1:00 and the boys had to get going to be at the field on time. As they ran out the door they asked their mother, if the coach asked us if we want to ride with him and "Pops" is it OK?

"Yes," replied the boys' mother, "But if you're going to be after 4:30 call me so I don't worry about you.

"Got it," said Billy, Love you Mom." And the boys and "Poodles" ran off toward the field.

When they got to the field they saw "Pops" sitting on the bench and ran "Poodles" right over to him. The old man rubbed the dogs ears and "Poodles' jumped up next to him on the bench. The rest of the team was arriving and as they came they would choose partners to play catch with. There were two boys that came every game and had to borrow a glove, the coach gifted them with Jakes and Jacks glove and the boys' broke into a glow, showing their delight in receiving the gifts. The boys looked at "Pops" and saw a big smile come over his face. They loved "Pops" and were glad to be his friend.

The coaches put their rosters together and took them to the Umpire who was standing behind the plate.

The Ump looked over the rosters and said, "Ok let's get these boys on the field and play ball."

The coach from the other team said, "Just a minute. The dog and the Old man are going to have to get off the bench and behind the fence. Only players and coaches are allowed in the dugout during the game."

The boys heard the coach say this and realized right off this would not be acceptable to them, even if the Old man was willing to make the move.

The coach asked the Umpire for his roster back, headed to the bench and approached the Old man. The boys were standing by as the coach started to talk.

"Sir," the coach said. There's a rule that says only players and coaches are allowed on the bench while the game is being played. I need to ask you to do something.

The Old man said, "I heard the coach from the other team. The dog and I can move. We don't want to disrupt the game."

"That's not what I wanted to ask you sir," said the coach. I wanted to let you know that I have been thinking about having an assistant coach for a long time. If it is all right with you, I would like to add you to the roster."

"It would be my honor to be your assistant coach," said the Old Man, but what about "Poodles?"

"Boys," he called out to the BBs. "Come over here with your friend and me. I'm in a bit of a pickle here, I need a pitching coach and you boys own the only one here I would trust this task to. Would you mind writing his name on the roster as the Pitching Coach? I would but you own "Poodles" and I think it would only be official if you boys put his name on the roster and both of you signed it."

The boys put "Poodles" name on the roster as pitching coach and both signed it. The coach took the roster to the Ump who was standing next to the other team's coach.

"Looks good to me," said the Ump, "Play Ball!"

"What," shouted the coach from the other team sharply? "They can't be coaches, or at the least the dog can't. I'm going to file a protest."

The Ump looked over at the Old man and the dog on the bench. Then he looked at Nate, and then in the eyes of the opposing coach.

"I understand," the Ump said, to the opposing coach.

"I thought you would see it my way, if the game was played under protest." the opposing coach replied.

"Yep," said the Ump. You file your protest, and when you fill it out, make sure you spell my name right. Now you coaches get your teams ready, and get them on the field.

And if any coach or player says another word about this while the game is being played, you'll be ejected. Except of course for the furry pitching coach, he can say anything he likes."

The BBs team had home field advantage so they took to the field. The coach gave "Poodles" the game ball, and gestured for him to give it to the pitcher. He did and the pitcher went to the mound and started warming up.

"Play Ball!" the Ump yelled again.

"Shoot the Mitt," yelled the old man. "Throw strikes. Make em swing the bat."

The parents in the crowed looked at him funny. None of the other parents were quite so vocal. Some of them were a little embarrassed for him.

The old man didn't care. He knew not everybody saw the game the same way and not everyone cheered on their loved ones the same way.

He hoped that the boys wouldn't be too embarrassed, but knew if they were they would get over it, and maybe someday get a chuckle out of it.

The game was close and the teams well matched. Both teams were hitting the ball, but with Billy at short and Bobby at second not many balls were getting out of the infield. Going into the top of the fourth the game was still scoreless. The BBs had turned a double play and that was pretty much the highlight of the game. But that didn't slow down the old man. He had a comment for every pitch and every at bat and half the calls. He loved baseball and loved to be part of the game.

Fifth innings came and went and then the sixth. The game only lasted 7 innings and both teams were expecting to see the game go into extra innings. Top of the 7th and still no score three, up and three down, the weakest link in the batting order leading off the bottom of the seventh.

First batter up goes down swinging. Second batter up and hits an easy grounder to the short. Third batter up, Tim Potoski, a big kid and a pretty good ball player, just hadn't had a lot of luck with the stick.

Good fielder and a great attitude. He was a right hander and had a tendency to take his eye off the ball just before it came to the bat. Being he was pretty good size the opposing team was playing him close to the line in left field and deep. The shift was on and right fielder was nearly playing in center.

First pitch a swing and a miss, second pitch a swing and a miss. There are two down in the bottom of the 7th and the pitcher had him down in the count. The next pitch came in on the outside of the plate and Tim swung the bat. It was a fast ball and he was just a little behind it, but he really cracked it. The ball tailed off into right field and followed the line. Tom was on his horse and rounding bases. The right fielder had a long way to get to the ball and the second baseman was headed to right field to line up for the cut-off. Tom rounded 3rd and when the ball the ball got to the cut-off man.

The cut-off man turned and hurled the ball to the plate, the catcher had the plate partially blocked but with a corner open. Tom went with a hook slide and toed the corner of the plate just as the catcher swept the tag.

"**Safe!**" The umpire yelled and spread his arms. The team and the old man jumped from their seats and roared in delight, "Poodles" yipped repeatedly in the excitement. The game was over and Billy and Bobbie's team would make it to the championships.

The boys lined up and passed the other team in line. Each team raised their right hands and congratulated the other with a slap.

Tommy ran back to the dugout and picked up the ball glove that had been gifted to him just before the start of the game. The name "Jake" written in magic marker showing him he had collected the correct one. A day Tommy would never forget.

The Letter

When all the celebrating at the field had been done and the players were done picking up, Billy, Bob, Pops and Poodles got into Nate's car.

"Who goes home first?" asked the coach.

"If it's all the same I would like you to take me home first." said the Old man. I have something that I would like to give to the boys to take home to their parents. They can come in with me and get it, won't take us more than a minute."

"Elm Street, it is," said the coach.

The old man could have asked him to take him to the moon and he would have done what he could to get him there. This was a big day for him, as well as for the boys and Tommy.

He had memories of the games he had played with Jack and Jake, being able to spend the ball game with their father, negotiating a deal for an assistant coach and a pitching coach, and last but not least, locking in a spot at the championships. This wasn't just a good day, this was a guided day, and he was grateful for every moment of it.

Nate pulled the car into the drive and Bobby said, "I'll wait out here with "Poodles". He won't understand if Billy, me and "Pops" all get out and leave him here alone with coach."

The coach understood where Bobby was going with this, but for some reason he couldn't keep it from rubbing him the wrong way. Not a lot, but still a sting.

Bill and the Old man walked into the house and on the table there was an envelope. The writing on the envelope said, "Benny and Barb Confidential."

"I need you to give this to your parents," said the old man. I will trust you not to open it. What they share of it with you is up to them, but I need your word that you will give it to them and do what you can to put it out of your mind. I know that is a hard thing to do, I have always been the curious type myself, but trust me. When the time is right and if the need arises they will let you boys know what I have written to them, if they don't you can trust there was no need."

"You have my word" said Billy. And Pops was right, his curiosity was peaked, but his word is his word and he would do what was necessary to make sure that the letter got to his parents unopened.

Billy started for the door. "See you Saturday "Pops." Be here about 10:15. We will bring lunch and plan on leaving about 5:00.

"And "Pops", he said. "Thanks for giving the ball glove to Tommy and Matt, and for coming to the game.

And for being the assistant coach and letting "Poodles" be the pitching coach. I love you "Pops" and so does Bobby and "Poodles"."

115

"I love you boys and "Poodles too." And you are welcome. I haven't had this nice a day since long before you boys were born. I'll see you Saturday."

Billy ran out the door letting it slam behind him. To the car with the envelope in hand and jumped in.

Bobby asked what was in the envelope and Bill said, "Not for us. When the time is right and if the need arises, mom and dad will let us know."

Nate started the car, backed out the drive, and "honked goodbye" to "Pops".

Soon they were home, and the coach let them out and honked good bye to the boys.

When the boys came into the house their mother was nowhere to be found. They ran into the living room and 'Poodles" ran up the stairs.

Their mother was upstairs getting ready for their father to come home. When she saw "Poodles" she yelled down the stairs. "Your dinner is in the oven. I'm getting ready for your father. "Date Night," she said.

"Got something for you from "Pops", Billy yelled up the stairs. "It's an envelope and only you and dad can read what is in it. We're going over there on Saturday, 10:00 to 5:00. I told him we would bring lunch."

"Put it on the dining room table and I'll get it when I come down," she replied."

Billy headed for the dining room and put the envelope on the table. Both the boys headed into the kitchen and grabbed forks and a knife from the silverware drawer.

Date night gave the boys the opportunity to tend for themselves. No spoons to them was ruffing it. They opened the oven door and saw their dinner, Lasagna, the favorite of both of the boys. They were not surprised, on date night everybody got something special. The smell when they had entered the door, had given them a clue to the oven's content.

Just when they had taken their dinner out of the oven and sat down to eat, their father broke through the door and passed them in a flash. "Date night" said their father as he ran up the stairs to shower, shave and put on a clean shirt, the boys looking forward to see if he would put a tie on. Date nights did not always require the same attire.

Soon both of their parents came down the stairs, stopped in front of the boys and asked. "How do we look?"

The boys looked at each other, crinkled their eyes and nose and casually said, "Good".

This being an expected response from the boys', no offense was taken.

"We have to go," said their father, "reservations at the "Embers", his wife's favorite restaurant.

Billy spoke up, "The envelope from "Pops" mom?"

"Oh yes," she replied and quickly went to the dining room, picked, up the envelope, went to the closet, opened the door, and reached up to the shoe box on the top shelf.

117

Without taking it from the shelf, she opened the box and slipped the envelope into the box.

"Got it," she said as she passed the boys in the kitchen and headed for the door.

"You boys know your bed time," the father said. Don't miss it, and make sure you say your prayers." Off they went on their date night.

After the boys finished their dinner, the plates went into the sink, and up the stairs with "Poodles" they went.

The boys lay in their beds looking up at the ceiling talking about the day, and how happy they were that Tommy had a chance to lead the team to victory. They laughed at how the coach and the umpire had handled the threat of protest by the other teams coach, and how the old man had announced the game to all that could hear from the bench.

They liked that their coach had referred to them as the "backbone" of the team and compared their play to Jack and Jakes, and what a good pitching coach Poodles had been.

But most of all, they talked about the generosity of their friend, and his willingness to give up his sons' baseball equipment to the players on the team that needed it. They wondered if that in some way had an impact on Tommy's home run, winning the game and moving on to the championships.

It was hard for the boys to fall asleep. One would say something and the other would turn it into a conversation.

"Coach played second base," said Billy.

"Yeah," replied Bobby. "That's why he gets so excited when we turn a double play. I bet he was pretty good. Not sure how he did with the bat though. When he was talking to "Pops" it sounded like he was the support for Jack and Jake."

"I don't know, I think that as good as Jack and Jake must have been they were probably team players. I bet they had the same respect for the coach as, the coach did for them," said Bobby.

"What do you think he meant when he told "Pops" he was sorry for his loss?"

"Something to do with them dying, we should ask "Pops," was the reply. "You think it's ok to talk to "Pops", about that? I wouldn't want to make him think about anything that's going to make him sad."

"Pops" said we could ask him about anything we wanted. He loves us and if he doesn't want to talk about it he'll tell us. I'd like to know what happened, and I'm sure you'd like to know too," said Bobby.

"We could ask the coach," said Billy. I bet he knows all about it. And I know if we asked him he'd tell us. I don't think he would feel bad about it."

"No," said his brother. "If I hear about it I want it to come from "Pops". It wouldn't be right to go around a friend about something like that. Whether it makes him feel bad or not, nobody knew Jack and Jake better than "Pops." If you don't feel comfortable about it I'll ask him.

He trusted us to go through all their stuff, so I think he would feel pretty comfortable with talking to us. We'll talk to him on Saturday if he hasn't got too much for us to do."

The boys' parents didn't get home 'till quite late. When they did they went straight to bed. The next morning when they went to the kitchen the boys wanted to know all about the special time their parents had the night before.

"First, we went to dinner," said their mother. "Your father had a steak with a baked potato, and salad. I had a shrimp cocktail and the sea food platter. It was very nice; we had a glass of wine and then went and saw a movie. Did you boys enjoy your lasagna?"

"It was great," said one of the boys. You and dad sure looked nice.

"Well, thank you," she replied. "You know as much as we love you boys, there are times that your father and I like to be alone. Besides it won't be long before you are grown and gone and have families of your own. Your responsibility will be to them. You see how little we see your grandparents." It's not that we don't want to be with them, but our duties are at home. When you get older you have to learn to be alone more and when you get much older, if you do, you will have to adjust to being by yourself. Life is change, and every day is its own gift. You have to adjust and find the joy, through the good and the bad. You boys are attached at the hip right now, but when you marry and have your families you'll find a way to adjust to being apart. It's life. Not always easy to understand but never without meaning."

"OK Mom." We're going to take "Poodles" for his walk."
And up from the table and off they went.

Their mother stood for a while with a blank look on her
face after the boys left. Having expected something a little
more meaningful than an "OK Mom" after sharing that
pearl of wisdom.

Saturday morning came around and the boys were looking
forward to what the day would bring. They knew there was
little left to be done in the garage, unless the Old man
would want them to put the treasures back into the boxes.
But neither of them thought that would be the request.

So the boys grabbed the lunches from the refrigerator,
thanked their mother for making them, hooked the leash to
Poodles and went on their way.

When they went around the house to the back door, they
saw that the garage was not opened. They knocked on the
door, and waited until they heard the Old man call them in.

The boys opened the door for "Poodles" and followed.
Billy went straight to the fridge and put the lunches their
mother had made for them on the center shelf.

"Sit down, boys," said the Old man. You know I haven't
stopped thinking about Wednesdays' game since you and
Nate dropped me off. The way you two turned that double
play, and that poke Tommy sent out to right field made the
game for me. I haven't been to a ball game in so long, and
to sit on the bench with you kids and 'Poodles, well I can't
get over it."

"We lay in bed and talked about it till way late, "said one of the boys.

"Really," said the Old man. You know it wouldn't surprise me if Nate did the same thing. His poor wife probably didn't get half a night's sleep. That was a pretty big deal to Nate you know. I bet that game filled a lot of dreams for him. I'm glad he came over and talked to me, and I'm glad to have been part of the decision to have you boys play."

The old man sounded like a kid that just hit his first home run.

"That pitcher of yours was sure throwing strikes, shooting the mitt. He's pretty good, not a lot of junk but he made them earn their hits." The old man carried on about the game and how Billy had scooped up the ground ball and flipped it to Bobby, Bobbies turn, and his shot to first base for the double play. He was reliving the game with every word.

"Tommy and Matt were sure glad to get gear," said Bobby. Neither of their folks has much, and they really love the game. It meant a lot to them, to have their own mitts. How come you didn't tell them they were from you?" It was hard for them to have to ask to borrow the other kids' mitts."

"Well boys," the Old man said. I didn't tell them they were from me because they weren't from me. They were from Jack and Jake.

122

They belonged to the boys; I just kept them in the garage until the right time came around for them to be used again. They seemed to fit Matt and Tommy, didn't they? Jack and Jake would have been glad to give the gloves to those boys."

"They fit them both just perfect "Pops", Billy said in a soft voice. "Pops, Bobby and I were talking last night and we wanted to ask you a question. We weren't sure if we should or not and we love you and neither one of us would ever do or say anything to hurt you."

"This sounds serious," said the Old man. "You told me the other day that you and your brother, and "Poodles" loved me, and I told you I loved you all too. And I told you awhile back you could ask me anything. You're not going to hurt me son. You go ahead and ask away."

"What happened to Jake, and Jack?" Billy asked.

"I figured the day would come when this would come up. Did you give the envelope to your mom and dad?"

'Yes sir," said Billy. I gave it to mom just before she and dad went on their date. I didn't open it or anything. Just gave it to her like you asked."

"Good," said the old man. And you've seen your mother since, and she didn't say anything about it?"

"No Sir, not a word," replied the boy.

"A date," said the old man. "I'll bet they got a kick out of that."

"Yes Sir," said Bobby. Actually I think my dad get more excited about it than my mom."

"That very well could be," said the old man through a chuckle.

"How about I tell you about what happened to Jack and Jake and Rusty and the Bride. We'll cover all the bases."

"To know what happened to my family I think you should first know them," said the Old man. "I'll do my best to describe them. If you have any questions, just ask and I will try to make things clear. When I was quite young I had to go into the service. The war in Viet Nam was going on and there was what was called a draft. We don't have one now but at that time all the young men, when they turned 18, had to register for the draft. You had a number pulled randomly and that was your number. It stayed with you and as the war went on, the numbers would go up and if the draft came up your number, you went. My number was called so I went. It was a hard time for me, and I had to do things and see things, I never thought I would have to. Anyway, I made it through and came home. I have a lot of mixed feeling about that time of my life, but when I got home, it put me in a time and place to meet my wife."

"I had gotten a job in a machine shop, and every day on my way to work I would stop at a little restaurant and have my coffee and a bite of breakfast. Behind the counter was the same girl every morning. Her name was "Julie". When she brought my coffee I would always ask for the sugar, and when she would bring it, I would just leave it sit. It was a big glass container with a silver lid and a cracker in it. When she brought the sugar I would order my breakfast, eat, leave a tip and go to the register to pay the tab.

Sometimes she would be working the register along with the counter and take the money.

One day after about two months of coming in, getting my coffee and asking for sugar, she laughed and said, "Why do you keep asking me to bring you the sugar, you never put any in your coffee."

"I told her that if I ever decided to ask her out on a date and things went well. When I walked her to the door, I wouldn't want to stumble over my words."

She said, "are you asking me out on a date?"

"Well," I said. "I'm thinking I might just get the practice in here, and try it out on another girl. Just in case things don't go well, that way I'll know what not to do if I ask you out."

"You don't get a lot of dates," She said confidently.

"Well," I said, "I had been gone a while, and I was kind of hoping that some nice girl would think I was irresistible and ask me out."

"And you think that's me?" she replied.

I told her "I didn't know, and asked if she was a nice girl, and if she found me irresistible?"

By that time, I had used up my breakfast eating time, and had to rush to get to work on time. So I threw a buck on the counter for the coffee, smiled and dashed for the door, not giving her time to answer.

The next morning I sat at the counter and she said, "So what time are you picking me up on Friday night?"

125

"Well," I said, "You find me irresistible. But how do I know you are a nice girl? "

"Don't press your luck," she said. "I'll be here at 7:30 on Friday night sitting at the counter. If you don't show up you'll have to find another place for breakfast."

"I'll be here at 7:30, I told her and I was. And we went on a date and we fell in love, and we got married and when we got married whenever I referred to her I called her "the Bride." And still do."

"We lived here in this house, and this was the only home we ever had. "It suited us just fine," he added. When Jake came along we set up his room right across the hall from ours. There are pictures in the living room of both the boys when they were first born. When we are done here, we can go out and look at them if you like.

"Jake was easy compared to Jack. When we first brought him home, he didn't cry much and when we put him to bed he would sleep pretty much strait through the night."

"I thought Jack's room was across from you and the brides'?" said Billy.

"It is now," said the old man. "But we had to make adjustments when Jack came along. He was a howler, that kid cried and cried and, when he quit crying it was only to rest up, for when he was ready to start crying again.

After a while, we decided that if Jake was going to get any sleep we would have to switch the boy's rooms.

We had one solid year of good sleep with a baby, before we had to make adjustments for Jack. The old man smiled.

126

He made it sound like it was a real hassle when Jack was born, but for some reason, he seemed to have fond memories of the additional effort it took with Jack.

"Kids grow up fast, and Jake and Jack did just that. You boys put me in mind of them in a lot of ways. They just fit together."

"They learned to read and share books, and when one of them got interested in something the other would follow in behind him. If one or the other didn't find it interesting, they would both drift away from it. It was like they were working off the same schedule."

"In about the second or third grade, Jake wanted to learn the flute. So Jack had to try it too. I don't remember which of them decided that the flute didn't suit them. But both their mother and I had a feeling of relief when we quit hearing the two of them trying to master it. We were glad they liked to read. Their mother had been a good reader but me not so much. It was easy for her to pick out classics and show them the fun in reading. I always had my mind going on something else. It was nice that their mother was able to provide. We balanced each other out pretty well. The books that you have placed on the front of the tables in the garage are yours. I'd like to say they are a gift from me. But I think it would be unfair to my wife, so they will be a gift from her. You don't have to take them with you today; you can do it when you feel the time is right."

"What about the Bible?" asked Billy.

"The Bible, you can take home today," said the Old man. "Why don't you run out and grab it now. I'll pull our lunch from the fridge and we can eat while we talk."

The old man pulled the keys from his pocket and handed them to Billy. "You can lock it back up after you get the Bible."

Billy took the keys and ran to the garage unlocked it, opened the door and pulled the light string.

He picked the Bible up from the table, turned to the door, pulled the string to turn off the light, swung the hatch tight over the loop and closed the pad lock. Keys in one hand and Bible under the other arm, he ran into the house letting the wooden door slam behind him.

The old man had gotten into the refrigerator and taken out the lunches. He put a carton of milk on the table and Bobby got 3 glasses from the cupboard. Billy sat down and laid the Bible in the middle of the table.

The old man bowed his head, "Thank you for these boys and for the food you have provided and the boys' mother has prepared for us. "In Jesus name we pray. Amen."

That was certainly a different prayer than the boys were used to hearing at lunch, but they appreciated that the old man had included their mother, for preparing what God had provided.

The three opened their lunches. Bologna and cheese with mayo and sliced tomato, a bag of chips and a cookie in each bag. It was a perfect lunch.

When they were about half way through their lunch, the old man got up and went to a drawer under the counter. He pulled out a pen and sat back down at the table.

"Pass me the Bible," said the old man.

Billy picked up the Bible and passed it on to the old man. He opened the cover and under Jack and Jakes signatures he wrote to "To my friends, Billy and Bobby, the BBs, Love "Pops," and under the "Pops" he wrote, "and my friend "Poodles". There he said, "Now the Bible is yours, I am happy to give it to you."

"Now where were we?" said the Old man. "That's right the books the boys read and shared. The books their mother and I had given them."

The Old man went on about how he and the boys would go to the park and play ball in the yard. "When we were at the park," he said. "There was a creek. They were small and we would find stones. The goal was to throw the stone across the creek. This was quite an event to them even though the creek wasn't more than 20 ft. across at its' widest point."

"We did this on Sundays," he added. "And would stop on the way home for Ice cream, the bride liked cherry chocolate chip if they had it. Everybody got one scoop."

"We took these park trips for years and as time went on the boys learned to skip stones, and would compete for the most skips. They would scour the riverbank looking for the flattest stones and pitch them side arm. Sometimes they would go quite a few skips before joining the other stones at the bottom of the creek."

"I would skip one myself and they marveled by the number of times and the lengths of the skips that came off my throws," he said.

"Later when the boys got older yet, we would take their ball, and gloves and I would hit them fly balls," he added. "They were both good ball players, and this was a big event. On Sunday afternoons, family times a ride in the car to the park, shagging balls and ice cream."

That's about the time we got "Rusty". The boys loved "Rusty" and he loved them. They liked to take him for a walk the way you boys do with "Poodles". He was a frisky dog and his long coat would shine, and blow in the wind. "Rusty" was their buddy, but they didn't mind sharing him with me. The bride would complain about the dog hair. But there was more than one occasion when she was caught rubbing that dog behind the ears and baby talking him, or slipping him a treat."

"The boys played catch on the driveway," he added. That's why the Garage door has wooden panels instead of glass. Either of the boys were known for a wild pitch every once in a while, and the glass turned into a difficult replacement to afford. I have to admit, I hit the panels myself a few times when we were playing together. It was a hazard of the game."

"They got good enough at baseball that they wanted to play organized ball, so the bride and I signed them up. She had more to do with them playing ball than I did. Washing uniforms, taking them to the games and dressing the wounds they had from sliding into bases."

"They were in their third year playing ball." The old man paused. "That's when Nate came in the picture, they ran together pretty close.

It was the best season they had had and they were getting down to the wire on whether they would make the championships and it came down to the last game of the regular season."

"The game was scheduled to start at 5:30 and it was a work day for me. So the bride was going to take the boys to the game and I was to meet them at the field at game time. Their mother got them ready and the boys put Rusty in the car. It wasn't but four miles to the park, he said." Anyway when they got to the intersection of Drake and Broadway they had a Green light, and their mother had just entered the intersection. A gravel truck, hit them broadside, all were killed except Jack, at the scene of the accident. When I got to the ball field there was a policeman that said he needed to take me to the hospital right away to see my son. I asked where his brother and mother were and he said he would talk to me on the way, but we must hurry. I was in a haze and got in the car. He told me of the accident and where it happened, and told me one of the boys was still alive but he was not sure of his condition. I asked which of the boys it was, and he said. He had no way of knowing."

"When I walked in the room," said the Old man. "I had to get up close to see that it was Jack. I looked at him for a long while, with tubes and bandages that had been soaked through with blood. I thanked God for not having taken him with his mother and brother."

About that time the Doctor put his hand on my shoulder and led me to a chair.

"I'm sorry for your loss" said the doctor. "But I have to tell you that your son, though able to make it here. May live for

131

a few days, his chances of survival are not in any way in our favor."

"I sat with him for a long time," he added, "Until I had to get out and catch my breath. When I got outside the room there was a young man that was dirty, and had greasy hands dressed in work clothes. He stood up when I came closer and asked me if I was the boys' father?"

"I replied to him that I was, and ask what I could do for him?"

"My name is Charlie said the young man, I'm so sorry sir. I was driving the truck, please forgive me?" The tears were running down his face and his hands were shaking.

"I don' know how I missed that light. I drive that road all the time. Nothing like this has ever happened to me before, I don't know what say."

"I looked at Charlie and could see his anguish, and hear the quiver in his voice. His pain was overwhelming."

"Charlie," I said. "Nothing like this has ever happened to me either. I could hear my voice quiver and feel my hands shake. I really don't know what to say." And I walked away feeling the tears roll down my face."

"I made my way to the cafeteria, got myself a cup of coffee, and sat for a short while."

"When I finished my coffee I went back toward Jacks room. Charlie was sitting in the chair in the hall his head in his hands."

"Come with me; I said, I would like you to meet Jack."

"I remember when Charlie got up his knees were weak," said the Old man. And he put his hand on my shoulder to steady himself. We walked into the room and pulled another chair close to the bed for Charlie."

"This is Jack," I told him, "my youngest boy."

"I would go home and rest and get up and go back to the hospital waiting for the inevitable,'' said the old man. "A week passed and no change, two weeks and no change. I prayed over Jack daily. And thanked God for taking his brother and mother quickly so they hadn't had to live through what Jack was going through. I felt guilty because I wasn't sure if I was grateful for them or for me. Finally, my prayers turned to thy will be done. Not because I wanted Jack to die. But because, if there was a time and a place and if it must happen, for me, this had become the time."

"Jack died the next day, said the old man. And we had the funerals and the team came and we marked the graves, and said our prayers and goodbyes."

"Was the Charlie we met the other day, the Charlie that was driving the truck?" asked Billy.

"One in the same," the old man said.

"How did you forgive him and become such good friends?" asked Bobby.

"I don't know if I ever did," said the old man. And I I'm not sure I ever needed to. My cross was the loss of my family. Charlie's cross was being responsible for their death. Over the years there were times I would wonder,

133

which of us had the greater cross to bear. To this day I am not sure, but I know we have both taken our lives forward, put our pain behind us and enjoyed beautiful lives, despite the crosses.

You will have your own crosses to bear in life. Find a place to store them and enjoy your life. I chose to store mine in my heart. God will help you carry them."

"Well now you know what happened. I'm about talked out," said the old man. "Why don't you boys take Poodles and your Bible home and I will see you again next Wednesday same time."

Billy and Bobby got up from the table and latched the leash on Poodles. Bobby picked up the Bible and asked the old man, "Are you sure he you want to give this to us."

"Sure as I'm sitting here," said the old man. "I'll see you Wednesday."

The boys walked out and headed for home. Both were very quiet, and both walked at a gate that was less aggressive than normal.

When the boys got home they walked into the kitchen and said, "Hello Mom."

"Your home a little early," she replied.

We had lunch with "Pops" and he told us about, His wife and Jack and Jake and Rusty; said Billy, as he set the Bible on the kitchen table."

"Pops" gave this to us," said the boys. "We're going to go upstairs. And the boys walked up the stairs, Poodles following behind.

Their mother looked at the Bible on the table and said, "I'll call you when dinner is ready." She opened the cover of the Bible and saw what had been written, "From Pops, to my friends Billy and Bobby the BBs. and Poodles." Instantly she thought of the envelope and went to the closet to pull it from the Box on the top shelf.

When she got it out, she saw that it was addressed to her and her husband and knowing he would soon be home, decided to wait for him to open it.

He came in the side door and said, "Anyone home. His wife called from the dining room, asking him to come in, and that she needed to talk to him.

"What's up Barb," he asked.

"Look at this," she said as she handed him the Johnson family Bible. "The boys brought it home with them. Ray gave it to them today. "There's a note to them on the inside cover. I really don't know what to think of it. Billy gave me this envelope before our date the other night and I had totally forgotten about it. She handed the envelope to her husband. He immediately said you haven't read what is inside?

"No," she replied, "I was waiting for you to come home and let you look at it with me." Benny opened the envelope and saw a letter. He unfolded it and read;

Dear Benny and Barb,

Thank you for sharing your sons with me. I wanted to let you know that the relationship with them has turned into something very special for me, and I believe for them and Poodles also.

The boys have become familiar with me and my home and have gone through items that had been personal possessions of my wife and sons. They were kind enough to take them from storage and put them in the garage on two tables they built, and I might add, did a very nice job on.

The point of telling you this is that I would like you and the boys to go through what is on the tables and take what may be of value to them.

My wife had some silver and china, and Barb, I thought you might enjoy having them. Your lunches have been a joy for us and I would like to show you my thanks with that gift from my wife.

There are some things I would like to discuss with the boys about my wife and boys, Rusty, and their deaths.

I would like the boys to know my family and the circumstances prior to and including the way they completed their journey here and started their eternal life. They were good boys like Billy and Bobby and Rusty was much like Poodles.

More important than wanting to talk to the boys, I would like to have your permission to do so. Death is a subject that is not comfortable with many people and if you would

*like to deal with their first personal encounter yourselves,
I would find it completely understandable. There are
details that I would reveal to the boys that are not only
personal but, knowing the boys, will. Impact them in their
visual minds and also their emotional perspective.*

*I came to terms with the loss many years ago, after
mourning the death of my family and adjusting to a new
life without them. It was difficult, but I have had a
wonderful life both prior to and after their passing. I
would do my best to allow the boys to know that life
allows us many challenges and there are crosses to bear.
But that life itself is our gift and that when God has
decided that your mission here is complete, your journey
home is reward. Even though the ones left behind, must
come to terms with the loss.*

*If I don't hear to the contrary, I will assume you have
read this and are good with me sharing this part of my life
with the boys.*

*I also need you to know that my time here is limited, and
soon I will, "God willing," see my reward.*

*I have no living relatives and what possessions I have,
were addressed in the first part of this letter. I have talked
to my good friend Charlie and anything that remains he
will deal with. Either with a sale or donation, we attend
the same church so nothing will go unused.*

*The house though is a different matter. In the envelope
with this letter is a card for an attorney, I have asked to
handle the sale of the house and a Trust for Billy and
Bobby, with what the house is able to sell for.*

As you are well aware, Billy and Bobby are very responsible and will I am sure by the time they are 18 be able to decide them-selves, what this money will be best spent on. Be it weddings or College, or the down payment on their own home or business.

With your permission I would like them to have total control of this and trust them to make their own decisions on how it will best suit their futures.

I, of course, have no objections, to you sharing this with them. You are wonderful parents and they are wonderful boys, I have come to love and trust them.

I would like to continue to see the boys, and I have asked Charlie to check in on us in case a need should arise that I am not able to deal with. Billy and Bobby know where the phone is and I am sure you have instructed them on calling 911 if something should come up.

If you have any questions or concerns, you can call me anytime or come to the house, I believe I have pretty much covered the bases.

The rocking chair, I would like to go to Charlie. It is old and worn but he has shared much time with me as I have used it and I know it would mean a great deal to him to have it. When the time is right, I will let him know that he is to have it.

Again, thank you for sharing what is dearest to you, with me.

My Best Regards

Ray J. Johnson

Benny shook the envelope and the business card fell out on the table.

"I'm not sure how to react to this," he said to his wife.

After not hearing a reply, he looked up at Barb and saw her wiping a tear from her eye. "I'm not sure either," said his wife. Put the letter in the envelope and the envelope in the Bible.

"I will get dinner finished up and call the boys down for supper. I would like to hear from them how their day went. They were pretty quiet when they got home."

The boys' mother got their dinner around and set the table, and called up the stairs for them to come down and eat. The dinner was the father's favorite dish and was served from the pot, on a pot holder with a large spoon. Everyone would serve themselves. This being the favorite of their father, he served himself first, and it was expected to be done that way whenever their mother served it.

The father took the ladle and carefully pulled 3 dumplings from the top of the pot. The dumplings covered what had cooked inside, carrots and potatoes, onion and chicken. After he ladled out the dumplings, it left just enough room to dip into the thick broth and well-cooked vegetables pulled out 2 scoops and put them on top of the dumplings.

The dumplings were soft but not doughy, and soaked up the gravy. This was something the boys had seen their father do on many occasions and loaded their plates exactly the same way.

It was obvious that the mother liked to make this for her husband and was always pleased to see how much he enjoyed it.

"Well, boys," he said, as he speared a carrot and potato for his first bite. "Did you get anything done at Rays today? Your mother showed me the Bible he gave you. That is quite a gift."

"Yes it is," said Billy, as he looked around the kitchen to find it. "Where did you put it Mom?"

"It's on the dining room table," said his mother.

Billy jumped up and ran to the dining room, picked up the Bible, set it next to his father and opened the cover.

"Look," he said. Pops put our names in it and everything, and signed it and even shared it with "Poodles. We didn't do much work today just mostly talked about his wife and sons."

He left the cover open and jumped back in his seat at table.

"How did that come up," asked the boys' father.

"We were talking about our baseball game and how Pops got to sit on the bench with Poodles, and how nice it was that he had gifted Jake and Jack's ball gloves to Matt and Tommy, and how much we liked to hear him yell at the game. Pops knows his baseball. We talked about how our coach and the umpire worked it out so Pops and Poodles could be coaches and sit on the bench. It was a really good time for Pops and he was glad to be able to be there."

"When we got done talking about the game, we told Pops that the night after the game while you and mom were on your date, we talked about asking him what had happened to Jack and Jake," said Bobby.

"We told him we didn't want him to talk about anything that would make him feel bad. He asked if I had given the envelope to our parents and I said we had. I told him I thought you enjoyed the dates with mom more than she did, and he laughed and said that he would be surprised if that was the case."

The boys' mother and father both laughed at "Rays" remark, and looked across the table at each other.

"He told us about when he first met his wife, when he came home from the service. She was a waitress in the restaurant where he would have breakfast every day. Her name was "Julie" and he told us how he got her to go on their first date together. I think he liked to tease her a little bit. Anyway they went on dates and fell in love and got married. He said that they lived in the same house he lives in now and that Jack was a real howler when he was a baby. For some reason or other he thought that funny cause he chuckled when he told us."

"Then he told us about how they had to switch Jack and Jake's rooms so Jake could get some sleep, and how Jack would rest from crying so he would have enough energy to cry some more."

The boys were playing a tag team with the conversation and one going on and the other adding detail to the subject.

"Pops has a bunch of books he wants us to have that he and his wife gave to Jack and Jake. We're going to get them there in the garage on the tables we made"

"He told us that the boys played the flute for a while, but I guess they weren't very good at it. And both he and his bride were glad when they decided not to play anymore. And they read and shared books and then got interested in baseball. They would play catch like we do in the back yard, but they played in the driveway.

Pops had to put wood on the door because the windows got knocked out. Jack played short and Jake played third.

Their mom would take care of their uniforms and make sure they got to the games on time, and Pops would meet them at game time and watch them play. That's how coach and Jack and Jake got to be buddies."

"All the boys had played together for 3 years and they had come to the last game of the regular season. The game was supposed to start at 5:30 and Pops was going to be there in time for the game to start. When he got there, a policeman was waiting at the field and told Pops he had to take him to the hospital right away. On the way to the hospital the policeman told Pops that there had been a bad accident and that one of his sons was the only one to survive and that he had to get him to the hospital right away. He explained that the car that his wife was driving got hit by a gravel truck that had run a red light. When Pops got to the Hospital, he went in to see which of the boys was alive and it was Jack, but the doctor told Pops that Jack was in bad shape and would not survive long. Pops sat with Jack for a long time and then had to catch his breath and went to the Cafeteria to get some coffee. That's when he met his friend Charlie."

"Did Charlie work at the hospital?" asked his mother.

"No," said Billy. He was driving the truck that killed Pops' family.

"And he and Ray became friends?" asked their father.

"Yes," said Bobby. Pops said he didn't know who had the heavier cross to bear, him, for losing his family or Charlie for being responsible for their deaths. He said that we all have crosses to bear and that he had stored his in his heart and over the years was able to pass the pain and live a happy life."

"Anyway," said Billy. Pops would go and see Jack at the hospital, and thank God that he took his wife and Jake quickly, sparing them the pain Jack had endured. He prayed that God's will be done, and soon after Jack died too."

"You boys had quite a day," said their father. "How was Ray when he was telling you about all this?"

"Pops is Pops. He told us he loved us and that he figured one day the subject would come up and he was glad to share it with us."

"How about you boys?" he asked. Are you doing ok?"

"Yea, we're good. Going to go and see "Pops" on Saturday."

The boys finished their dinner, collected their plates, put them in the sink and headed for their room.

When the boys had gone to their room their parents sat at the table quietly thinking of what they had just heard. The way the boys had described the day and the comfort they seemed to feel in knowing what had happened to Rays' family.

"I don't have any issue with what Ray discussed with the boys," said the father. In fact, I don't know how it could have gone any better. I'm glad that we didn't read the letter before the boys were told, I think I may have tried to guide them through it. It was best that it happened the way it did."

"What about the boys going to Ray's knowing he is not well?" asked Barb.

"Let it play out," said Benny. "The boys will do the right thing if something comes up. And Ray said in the letter that he had Charlie keeping an eye on him. I wish I had more time with Ray myself. I think he would have been a good friend."

Saturday came around and the boys were up, had their breakfast and gathered hooked up Poodles. They set off on their walk over to see the old man, moving at a pretty good clip, excited about the day. When they turned on to Elm, they could see and ambulance in the drive at the old man's house.

They walked up the drive slowly, not knowing what to expect and saw the old man lying on a stretcher being loaded into the ambulance. Charlie was standing next to him and motioned the boys to come over to their friend.

144

Pops looked at the boys and said, "Looks like we're going to have to make other plans," raised his right arm and pointed with his index finger to the sky.

"Ok," said the boys. And they watched as Pops went into the ambulance and it slowly drove away.

"What's wrong with Pops, Charlie?" asked Billy.

"He's just worn out," said Charlie. He's ok though, he wouldn't want you boys to worry about him."

"We're not," said Bobby. "Where are they taking him?"

Charlie pulled a card out of his pocket and handed it the boys. "You take this and give it to your parents," he said. They'll be able to take you to see him. I'm going up there now."

The boys turned around and started walking back home. Billy was clinching the card in his hand. Neither spoke but Poodle kept pulling in the opposite direction, as if to tell them that they were going the wrong way.

They wanted to get home as soon as possible so their father could take them to see Pops. As they walked up the drive they could hear the lawn mower in the back yard.

They passed the side door of the house and headed straight out to get to their father. He was about half way done with the yard and turned the mower off when he saw the boys, knowing they should be at Ray's and not home.

"Hey dad," asked Billy, "Can you take us some place right away?"

He handed him the card and his father read it.

"Charlie gave us that when we got to Pops house, and there was an ambulance there. He said what's on the card is where they were taking Pops."

"Sure boys," said their father. "I can take you. Let me go inside for a minute and see if your mother might want to go too."

The boys' father went into the house and handed the card to his wife. "I'm taking the boys to see Pops. Would you like to go?

"Are you sure that's what you want to do?" asked his wife.

"No," said her husband. But I'm sure that's what the boys want to do. I don't have any details so I think we should leave right away. Do you want to come?

"Yes," she said, and followed her husband out the door.

They got in the car, and Poodles came along.

"I don't think Poodles will be able to come in," said the boys' father.

"Pops "will want to see him," said one of the boys. "We'll find a way to work it out."

They hadn't driven very far and their father pulled into a circular drive. In the center of the circle was a big brick wall that stood all by itself. It had plain letters on it that said Trinity Hospice.

The writing and the wall were the same as what was on the card that Charlie had given them.

Their father parked the car and all got out, the boys with Poodles on his leash.

"I think you should leave Poodles in the car, said the boys' father I am sure they won't let him come in."

"Pops is going to want to see him," said Billy. "It will work out."

The father thought hard about this and though against his better judgement, let the boys make the decision to bring Poodles in, knowing it would cause pain to the boys if Poodles was denied access.

The family walked to the front door. It was a double door and there were wheel chairs on the right and another set of double doors before entering the lobby.

At the right side of the lobby there was a counter with a lady sitting behind it, and on the counter, there was a book for visitors to sign in. There were long hallways that went off like fingers in three directions, and there were rooms equally spaced on either side of the halls. It had carpet and was very quiet. There were some older people in the center where there were couches. Some of them sat in wheel chairs.

"We are here to see Ray Johnson," said Billy, to the lady behind the counter.

"And these are your parents?" she asked in a soft voice.

"That's fine," she said. They will have to sign in for you and escort you to Mr. Johnson's room. The dog will have to go outside. No pets are allowed in the facility."

"But Pops is going to want to see Poodles," said Billy.

"I'm sorry," the woman said. "But those are the rules."

Just then they saw Charlie walking up the hall to the desk.

"Hi boys," said Charlie, these must be your parents. Would you like to introduce them to me? He knelt over and patted the dog on the head "Hi Poodles." he said.

"Sure, Charlie," said Billy Mom and Dad this is Charlie. Charlie, this is my mom and dad, Benny and Barb."

"They are here to see Mr. Johnson." I was just telling them they would have to take the dog outside. "No pets are allowed in the facility. Their parents are signing them in."

"No exceptions." said Charlie.

"I understand," He said in a voice that made him appear to be angry.

He said nothing more and walked out the double doors, and looked at a sign above the wheel chairs. It read, "To be used by staff only."

He took one of the wheel chairs and walked by the desk.

"Sir," the woman said. Did you not see the sign?

"My name is Charlie, sign me up as a volunteer," he said sharply and kept walking.

The lady behind the counter appeared to be pretty mad about it, and was dialing numbers on the phone.

The boys saw Charlie push the wheel chair into a room down the hall. Pops was lying in the bed when Charlie entered, "somebody here to see you pops." If I help you can you get into the wheel chair?"

The old man looked drained but said, "with your help I am sure we can work it out."

Charlie gently picked up the old man and put him in the chair, adjusted the foot rest so his feet wouldn't drag and made him as comfortable as possible. Two men walked in the room just as Charlie started to walk the old man out.

"We'll have to put him back in the bed and take the wheel chair," said one of the men.

"I understand," said Charlie. In a very direct voice, as he pushed the old man past the two men and down the hall, the men following.

One of the men said, "Sir you have to stop and let us take the old man back to his room".

"I understand," said Charlie in the same tone. The old man chuckled, at his perseverance.

"Poodles" was tugging at his leash as the old man approached. When he was just a few feet away, Bobby let the leash go. Poodles ran and jumped on the old mans' lap, licking his face and wagging his body along with his tail.

Just then another man came walking up; he had a suit and a tie on.

149

The woman stood up and said, "This man just took a wheel chair and went and got Mr. Johnson and brought him out here to see this dog. After I politely told him there were no pets allowed."

Charlie put out his hand to the man in the suit, looking him dead straight in the eye said, "Hi I'm Charlie, the new volunteer."

By this time there was quite a crowd and a policeman was walking in the front door. He saw the dog on the old mans' lap the boys, and their parents, and smiled.

"I called," said the woman behind the desk. This man has shown total disregard for the rules of this facility and needs to be removed."

"Which man would that be?" asked the Policeman.

"That would be me," said Charlie, "The new volunteer".

"Volunteer?" said the Policemen. "I guess I don't see the problem."

"He just made himself a volunteer so he could take the wheelchair," said the woman behind the counter.

"I see so he made himself a volunteer, and went and got this wheel chair so he could bring this gentleman out to see the dog. It seems to me that there is only one reasonable thing that can be done in this situation," said the policeman.

"And what would that be?" said the woman.

"Well seems to me," the officer said. "The only way to make things right, is to make the dog a volunteer."

Everyone looked at the policeman surprised. Wanting to hear what would be said next and by whom.

"That's ridiculous," said the woman. "I have half a notion to call your sergeant and file a complaint."

 "I understand," said the policeman.

"I thought you would see it my way after I mentioned filing a complaint," she replied.

The policeman pointed at the name tag above his badge, "You see this mam? When you file your complaint make sure this name is on it, and make sure you spell it right."

Just then the boys and Pops too, recognized the policeman. He was the umpire from their ball game. The three of them smiled at each other.

The man in the suit stepped in. This was the kind of thing that would not sit well for the facility if it got into the papers or on the news, rules or no rules.

"I think the option you have presented is reasonable, he said. So as of now Charlie and………….

"Poodles," the old man said.

"Charlie and Poodles are officially volunteers. "Poodles will have access to Mr. Johnsons' room as long as he is here. Thank you for your assistance officer. Is there anything else that needs to be said?"

"Not unless the furry new volunteer has something to say," said the officer.

Everyone, but the lady behind the counter chuckled, and went their way. Charlie pushed the old man to his bed, and the two men helped him in. "Poodles" the boys and their parents, sat in the room waiting for the old man to get comfortable.

They all sat and talked. Mostly about their friendship and what had taken place over the last few weeks. Barb told the old man what a wonderful gift the Bible was.

She told the Old man about the shoe box and what was in it, and added that the letter from him would go in there also.

After a while, the Old man said, "I am getting tired and need to get some rest. Before you leave I would like to pray with all of you."

Charlie and the boys and Barb and Benny all put a hand on the old man, closed their eyes and bowed their heads.

"Dear God," the old man prayed. "Thy will be done. In Jesus name we pray. Amen."

Everyone said, "Amen", and filed out the door. The old man held his right arm up index finger pointing to the sky.

When the boys got back in the car their father suggested that they get a pizza and take it home. So they could all sit together and talk about the day.

They stopped at "Pennies", a local pizzeria that everyone liked. The dad went in and got a small peperoni for the Boys and a deluxe for him and Barb. They had gone there many times before with their cousins, and grandparents and everyone always enjoyed the food and the time together.

When they got home, the boys' mother took paper plates from the cupboard and opened the pizza boxes.

Billy bowed his head and said, "God is great God is good we thank him for this food, by his hand we all are fed we thank him for our daily bread. Thy will be done. In Jesus name we pray, Amen."

"That was a very nice prayer, said Bills' mother. You never added thy will be done to it before was there a special reason?"

"Pops is dying," he said, I hope that "Gods will" is to take him peacefully. Whatever way it goes, I wanted to let God know everyone is ready."

"Thank you, Billy, said Bobby."

The boys ate their pizza, and the table was quiet. The father had expected to have to prepare the boys for what was to come, but realized it had been taken care of. When they were finished, the boys went to their room with Poodles and went to bed.

The next morning was Sunday and the family went to church. The boys sat on either side of their parents. The sermon was long and loud and formal. Many prayers were said, and at the end of each one both of the boys added "Thy will be done," in recognition to Pops.

After the service was over, their father offered to take them to see "Pops" as it was on the way.

At first the boys weren't sure if it would be a good idea being Poodles was not along. But as they got closer they decided to stop and say "hello".

153

They all got out of the car and headed in, expecting to face the lady that had objection to Poodles, only to find another woman behind the counter.

"We stopped to see Mr. Johnson," the boys' father said, to the lady behind the desk.

"Mr. Johnson is no longer with us," said the lady. "He passed in his sleep last night. A man named Charlie was notified. He left this number if anyone stopped by."

The woman passed the note across the counter and gave it to the boys' father.

"I am sorry for your loss," said the lady. "Is there anything I can do for you?"

The boys looked at their father, and then at the lady, and shook their heads slowly, "No."

The family made their way to the car, got in, and sat for a minute in silence.

The father started the car and backed out. Making his way home, "I'm sorry Ray died alone," said the boys' mother.

"He didn't," said Billy. "He had Jake and Jack and his wife, and Rusty and me and Bobby, and Poodles and Charlie and Nate in his heart. He had all the company he needed."

"Are you boys alright?" asked their father.

"No", said Bobby. But in time we will be. Pops said it takes time to move someone you love into your heart. I feel real bad cause I won't see him again. But, God willing, he will get his reward now. We won't ever forget him. He'll just move into our hearts."

"What's on the paper that Charlie left?" asked Bobby.

"It's the name of the funeral home they took Ray to. There will be an obituary in the paper. It will tell us when there will be a viewing and about the funeral. You will be able to see him before he is buried. You haven't done that before, but your mother and I will be with you."

The rest of the day was quiet and the boys stayed close to Poodles and the house. There was no Sunday dinner, but their Mom made the boys sandwiches. Bologna and cheese with mayo and a slice of tomato.

Benny and Barb talked about the day and what was best to do with the upcoming days.

"I think we should give the boys the letter from Ray," said Barb. "Before the funeral, and let the boys know what he had been thinking about."

"We can do it at breakfast tomorrow morning. I will make sure the boys are up early. We can do it before you go to work."

They put the Bible in the kitchen on the table. The letter was still in it, and both went to bed in anticipation of what they were hoping to be a comforting morning for the boys.

The night went fast and there was a lot of interruption in the sleep of both of the boys' parents.

They were torn between the joy of showing the boys how Ray felt about them, and how it could magnify the loss, as

155

the boys dealt with it. Either way they knew in their hearts it was the right thing to do and after getting up an hour early, dressing and getting breakfast prepared went in to wake the boys.

Poodles was confused by the change in routine and quickly jumped up on the boy's beds, back and forth, waking them and making the first difficult task of the day bearable.

The boys pushed Poodles away and got under the covers. But Poodles would have no part of it. He knew by the presence of the boys' parents that there was a need for the boys to get up, and he would find a way to get these boys around. And do it in a way that got him some attention.

First Billy threw off his covers and hugged Poodles. Roughly playing with him, letting him know he was getting up. When he let go, Poodles jumped to Bobbies' bed and wrestled and pulled at the covers until, Bobby gave in to the pressure and responded as his brother had.

They saw their parents standing at the door way.

"Your mother has made an early breakfast boys," said their father. "Do what you have to do and go down stairs, you can change your clothes after you eat."

This was in no way part of the normal routine. The boys jumped from their beds and took to the bathroom to clean up, and do their business.

They were done quickly and went to the kitchen to the smell of sausage and eggs, their plates sitting on the table next to each other and the Bible sitting in front of their plates.

"If you open your Bible, in the center you will find something we think you should read," said their mother.

The boys pushed their plates to the side, leaving a space big enough to pull the Bible toward them and open it.

The envelope left enough of a gap in the binder that it opened naturally to the location of the letter.

They put their heads together and read it at the same time, one boy holding one side of the letter, and the other boy holding the opposite side.

Their mother watching intently seeing the shape of a heart with the boys' heads touching, their outside arms angled to the letter and Pops' letter completing the figure.

The boys read the letter taking their time. In fact, enough time that they may have read it more than once.

When they were done, they placed the letter back in the Bible and closed it, pushed it back to the center of the table and pulled their plates in front of them.

Their parents were at a loss for words, wanting to say something but not having a clue of what it would be. Watching the boys read the letter and seeing their reaction puzzled them. It was a moment between the boys and they weren't sure if they should be included in it.

"I'm glad Charlie will have Pop's chair," said Billy.

"Yea, me too," said Bobby. "We should have Charlie help us go through the garage too, I guess we can do that after the funeral."

"Mom," said Billy. We have a spare wall in our room. When we get to Pops house, maybe you can help us take the pictures down, and we can set them up the same way here. We can put Jake and Jacks books in the book shelf in the living room."

"Whatever you like boys, your father and I can help you. Just tell us what, and how you would like it to be done," replied their mother.

"The viewing is at 10:15 on Wednesday," said the father, "and the funeral will be right after. I will take off work and we can go together."

"Thank you, Dad," said the boys, quietly finishing their breakfast excusing themselves from table and heading for their room.

Billy stopped and turned to his parents, "We forgot to say our prayers before breakfast," he said.

"I think that base was covered Billy," said his dad. You and your brother have a good day and I will see you when I get home from work."

The boys continued up-stairs to get dressed and start their day. Thinking it would be good to get their chores out of the way, and prepare for Wednesday.

"Those are some good boys" the father said, as he opened the door and headed for work.

Their mother sat at the table, feeling the pain of her boys, but knowing they would be all right.

The boys concentrated on their chores and were together for the rest of the day. Tuesday was much the same. They didn't take their walk with Poodles and had to take the leash from him and hang it on one of the coat hooks, to keep it out of his sight.

Wednesday came quickly and the boys' mother had their clothes laid out. They were the same clothes that they would wear to church, dark pants blue shirt and dark tie. The two boys cleaned up well and at about 10:00 were ready to go.

They put Poodles on his leash and made their way with their mother and dad to the car. Their father was not sure how things would go with Poodles, but this was not the time to make objections or suggestions. They got in the car and had a silent ride to the funeral home.

When they got to the funeral home, Charlie and one of the directors met them at the door. Charlie leaned over to pat Poodles, and greeted the boys by name, not sure which was which.

There was a pedestal with a book that looked like the one at the hospice. Each of the four in the family signed their name. Billy wrote Poodles on a separate line if his own.

There were quite a few names on the register, but none that the boys recognized. They walked down a hall to some double doors. In front of the doors on an easel was the Picture of Pops when he was in the service.

There was a small dark engraved sign under the picture. "Ray .J. Johnson" was all it said. Next to the picture was a box with plastic coated copies of the Obituary that had been posted in the paper. The boys' mother took five from the box and put them in her purse.

The room was long and had chairs in the middle, maybe 30 or 40, and on either side of the chairs there were couches and cushioned chairs. The pictures from the wall at Ray's house were on another easel that was setting next to the head of the casket.

The boys' parents led the boys and Poodles to the casket and stood on either side of the boys. Poodles rose and put his front paws on the side. Billy gently made him get down and sit. Poodles' tail wagged, but he sat still as directed. The family bowed their heads and silently said prayers for the old man.

When they were finished they passed to the left so others could approach and pay their respects.

The boys showed their parents the pictures of Jack and Jake and the old mans' wife. Charlie walked up while they were talking about them.

"If you want, you can have these," said Charlie. "Let me know and I will make arrangements with the director to box them for you bring them to your house."

"Yes," said Bobby. "We have a wall that we would like to put them on in our room. Mom said she would help us. Who are these other people?"

"Mostly they're people from the Church and some who worked with Pops. They are all very nice, I don't know how many will be coming to the cemetery. Will you and your family be going?" asked Charlie.

"Yes," said Bobby, "And Poodles too."

"Pops" would like that," Charlie replied. "Maybe tomorrow we can go through some of the things in the garage, your mom and dad can come if they like. If you don't mind I can help you see what there is you would like to keep."

"That would be fine," said the boys. "We were hoping you would be there with us."

Charlie turned away and took a seat in the front row. "You and your family sit up front with me," he said."

Charlie pulled the seat that was second down from him out and put it aside. "This will be just enough room for Poodles. You boys can sit on either side of him," he said in a soft voice.

The minister from Pops Church made his way up to the front of the room, to a podium that was set up next to easel with the pictures. When he stepped behind it everyone made their way to the chairs in the center of the room.

The minister said a prayer that Pops be accepted, and find peace, in the presence of God. And, that we were there to celebrate his life. After he spoke, he asked if anyone would like to say anything.

Charlie stood up and stepped up beside the preacher.

"I just want to thank Pops for being the best most accepting friend a man could ask for. There are three other of his friends here that are welcome to say something if they like."

Charlie gestured to the boys'. They both bowed and shook their heads "no." All that needed to be said was done so with Pops when he was living. They were at ease with what Charlie had said.

The preacher said a few more words and mentioned a luncheon in the basement of the Church after the funeral. He closed the ceremony and asked us to file out from the front row to the back. There was music playing, "Rock of ages". It was nice to hear it and it felt warm to the boys.

The boys made their way to the cars that were lined up. There was a black limousine right behind the Hearst that would carry Pops.

Charlie motioned to the boys, their parents and Poodles to get in. He took the car behind the limousine.

The procession started and the moved slowly through town, down Broadway. The boys took notice of the intersection of Broadway and Drake. They both closed their eyes and prayed as they went through the intersection.

They drove on, and when they got to the outside of town they saw the cemetery and gravesite from the road.

The Hearst pulled up close to the gravesite and there were 6 men that approached the rear of it. The driver got out and opened the rear door. The pall bearers pulled the casket to the grave and set it on top of the open grave, with long bronze rods with balls on the ends and straps across to hold the casket.

They carried Pops to the grave and placed the casket in position.

Everyone waited patiently for the procedure to be completed. There was a pile of dirt on the opposite side that was covered by a large blanket.

The Minister came to the side of the grave and said a prayer and closed the ceremony. Everyone filed by the casket, some touched it and others stopped shortly and bowed their head.

This was the last good-by and the boys and Poodles stood at the end of the grave waiting for everyone to pass by.

The boys and their family made it back to the limousine and they were taken back to the Funeral Home. Charlie followed behind and when he arrived got out and walked the family to their car.

"Did you want to come to the luncheon?" asked Charlie.

"Would it make it easier for you Charlie?" asked the boys?

"Either way," he said. I will be fine.

"Then I guess we'll just go home," said the boys. "What time you want to meet at Pops tomorrow?"

"How about 10:15," said Charlie. "Perfect," said the boys. And the three of them raised their right arms, and pointing their index fingers to the sky, went their separate ways.

Benny took another day off from work, for his boys. He had some vacation time built up. He was the type to hold it until he couldn't use it. His wife never quite understood that, but she was not aware of the environment or her husband's daily routine, and didn't view work the same way as her husband. She was grateful for his decision, as were the boys.

They all were around by ten and made their way to Pops' house. Charlie was there to meet them. The garage opened and the house unlocked. He had a pick-up with a trailer on it and was ready to take the remaining articles to the church. He had un-assembled boxes next to the counter in the kitchen with two rolls of box tape.

There was a fresh stack of boxes in the garage with two more rolls of tape. He had the boxes the boys had taken the treasures from in a pile in the fire pit, and planned on burning them when the task was complete.

The boys' family and Poodles got out of the car and approached Charlie in the garage.

"You'll find boxes and the box tape needed to assemble them all around the house. I have blue tags and green tags. The blue tags are for you, and the green tags will be for the church. They have worked things out with a number of families that can use household goods, and the rest will go to the Goodwill.

"Pops" said to tell you not to be shy about taking what you want and not to feel bad about leaving anything that might serve others' needs."

"You must have started early," said Billy.

"Pops and I started this a long time ago," said Charlie. "Try to enjoy yourself and when you are done we will call a couple of guys I know from the Church to help me load the rest into the trailer."

"Your dad and I can put the things you want in the back of my truck and take them to your house. We have all the time in the world," he added. Barb, you and Benny can start in the kitchen. I think the boys and I will have our hands full in the garage," said Charlie.

Benny and Barb walked into the house. Benny pushed on the wooden door to make sure it wouldn't close on his heels. The door slammed with a bang, and the boys looked at each other and smiled.

"We have to get the books," said Billy.

"This is how you make the box," said Charlie. He opened the flattened folded box, made the folds all the way around and secured the bottom with two layers of box tape.

"Got it," said the boys. And they put together four boxes.

The boys started collecting the books from the table and putting them into the boxes. Charlie went along the wall and picked up a weed whacker, rakes and shovels. He asked the boys if they thought their father or they would have a use for them.

The boys declined and Charlie carried them out to the trailer.

"There's a snow blower, and lawn mower," said Charlie.

"You can ask dad but I am sure he won't want them. He has his own, and Mom gave him his snow blower, for some reason or other it seems to mean a lot to him," the boys replied.

"We're going to takes Pops fishing stuff, unless you can use it," said Billy.

"No," said Charlie. I have my own line and a pole. Pops would like you to have his tackle box and the like, put it in the back of the truck."

Charlie got to the work bench and asked the boys if their father would like any of Pops tools.

Billy ran in the house and asked his dad.

His father shook his head no without saying a word, and Billy ran back to the garage letting the door slam behind him.

When he got back to the garage Charlie was picking up the old man's hammer and just about to put it into the box.

Bobby shouted out, "No!" Billy and I need the hammer, and the tape measure, and the steel yard stick.

"Ok," said Charlie. "Is it ok if I put it in the box with his fishing tackle?"

"Sure, said the boys. "But we can't forget those."

"The boys put the toys in a box of their own and put a green tag on it. There will be some kids that will be glad to have these," they said.

166

Charlie took the box of silver and the one with china and put it in a separate box, with a blue label, pulled a marker from his pocket, and wrote "Barb" on it.

The garage cleared out quickly, until there were only the tables the boys had made.

"Would you boys mind if I took these tables and put them in my garage?" asked Charlie.

Billy and Bobby looked at each other and said, "That would be great Charlie. Don't forget the rocking chair. I know Pops would want you to have that."

"Thank you boys" said Charlie. "When I call the guys from the church, we can dismantle the tables. They are marked well and I will be able to nail them back together just like you did."

The boys smiled. They could see the kindness that Charlie was showing them in his efforts to help to collect treasures.

The three of them finished up in the garage and made their way into the house.

The boys' parents had pretty much collected all that was in the kitchen. All of the boxes were full and the cupboard doors open. There was nothing left to go through and the boxes all had green tags.

Charlie had emptied the refrigerator, unplugged it, and put a pan under the freezer to collect the water that would accumulate from the frost.

Billy said, "Where are the Iron skillet and the coffee pot?"

167

"They're in this box," said their mother.

"We're going to have to put those in a different box and put a blue tag on it," said Billy.

Bobby went to the open refrigerator and pulled down the aluminum ice cube trays, "we need these too," he said.

"Ok," said Charlie, "They're yours, let's go upstairs and you can look through it and see if there is anything that you need up there."

The boys led the way, through the archway and pass the buffet and empty wall. The rocker was in its rightful spot and the davenport shined with the plastic cover. Billy opened the door to the upstairs and walked up slowly. When he got to the top of the stairs, he made his way into the first room on the right.

"This is Pops and the Brides room," he said to his parents.

The room was as bare as when they had first seen it, but the picture of the Old Mans' wife was not on the night stand. It was with the others that were displayed at the funeral home.

Charlie put a green tag on the bed and the night stand, Ok with you Boys?" he asked?"

"Perfect," the boys replied.

The boys' parents were silent. Honored to be part of the event, and proud of the way the boys were handling the needs of the situation.

Bobby led the way to the bathroom, and said, "Nothing here."

This left Jake and Jack's rooms. The boys stopped at the door, they had never been in these rooms and were not sure what to expect, and weren't sure if they should open the doors. They looked up at Charlie, he nodded his head yes. And the boys opened Jakes door.

The room was set up much like, the Old Man and his wife's room. With dormers and windows that let the light shine in. The room was bright and there was no need to turn on the light.

The rooms had always been a mystery to the boys and they had imagined all sorts of different things about them and their contents.

The boys looked intently around the room and walked to the closet and opened it, to see what was inside.

The rooms were empty except for a bed and an empty dresser. The closet held nothing.

The boys looked at each other and smiled, knowing the old man had shared all of his sons' treasures with them.

Charlie asked, "Green tags OK with you boys?"

"Perfect:" the boys said. And they walked out the room. "Poodles" followed along, looking around and sniffing like he was trying to find something. You could tell he wanted to see the old man. But couldn't quite figure out where he was at.

Billy opened Jack's door directly, and made the same walk
through, smiling with his brother. Charlie tagged the bed
and dresser.

"There's the buffet and the davenport in the living room,"
said Charlie.

The boys looked at their parents and said, "I think a green
tag for them."

Their parents nodded in agreement, and asked the boys if
they minded riding home with Charlie.

The boys said, "No" and their parents walked down the
stairs with Poodles, the boys, and Charlie, close behind.

Benny looked at Charlie and said, "You and the boys take
all the time you need," and left.

Benny picked up the box with the skillet, coffee pot and ice
trays and took it to the car.

Charlie and the boys sat at the yellow kitchen table with the
shiny padded chairs and shiny steel tube legs.

"I'm going to green tag this table and the chairs," said
Charlie.

The boys nodded in agreement.

The three of them sat silent for some time.

Bobby bowed his head and said, "God is great. God is
good. Thank you for "Pops". Thy will be done. In Jesus
name we pray. Amen".

The three of them rose from the table.

"Do you boys and Poodles need to take another walk through?" asked Charlie.

"No" said the boys, "But could we drive by the ball field on the way home, we don't have to stop."

The three of them with the pitching coach walked out to the truck, jumped in and made their way past the ball field and to the boys' house.

They pulled the boxes from the back of the truck and took them into the house. Charlie grabbed the books, and the boys asked him to put them in the living room next to the book shelf.

The boys took the books from the box and placed them on the shelf, keeping them all together on their own shelves. This would be their spot.

Billy called out for his parents.

"We're up here in your room," replied their mother.

Poodles, the boys and Charlie, all walked up stairs.

"The funeral home dropped these off," said their father. "We were just finishing up hanging them. Is this the way you wanted them?"

"Perfect," said Billy. They looked at Charlie and he smiled with approval.

"Let's go down stairs and have something to drink and sit at the kitchen table" said the boys' mother. I may have some snacks we can chew on too.

Everything had gone smoothly. They had been guided through the day and found pleasure in each other's company, and their memories of the old man.

They sat at the kitchen table.

Charlie, would you like coffee?" Barb asked, "The boys will have milk and I have a pot made up."

"That would be fine, black please. Thank you," he replied.

She reached into the cupboard and pulled out some windmill cookies, put them in the center of the table, walked into the other room opened the closet and pulled the box from the top shelf. She picked up the Bible from the dining room table brought both out and placed them next to the cookies and sat down.

Nothing was said by anyone for a while, the cookies were passed around and the coffee and milk were started on.

The boys' mother removed the lid from the box, and then opened the Bible to where the envelope from the old man was placed.

"I have memories of you boys, in this box," said their mother. "And I am the keeper of these memories. I am going to put this letter from Ray in the box, and on your eighteenth birthday the two of you can open the box and every sealed envelope, and read them. If I am not here than you will share this time with your father, as you continue to grow I will continue to ask you to write down what you see."

"Charlie, you are invited to this event."

172

"These will be memories you can share if you are gifted with children. "

"Thank you," said Charlie, "I will look forward to being here."

Their mother placed the envelope from the old man in the box, put the lid on, and carried it to the closet, placing it on the top shelf.

Charlie rose from the table. Thanked them for allowing him to be part of the day, and raised his right arm index finger pointing toward the sky. The boys did the same.

As he left he told the boys that he would be sharing time until that special meeting with them, and would look forward to being part of the continuing experiences of their lives. Everyone went their separate ways. The boys went to their room with Poodles, Benny and Barb to their daily duties, and Charlie to his future with Pops in his heart.

The End

Dear Lord;

Thank you for all my gifts.

My mother, my father my brother, Cindy, Connie, Heather and Hollie, Heather Elaine, all of my Grandchildren, all of my extended family, and all my dogs. My pain and my heartache, my joy and my sorrow. With your grace, may they all be tools that I need to serve the work you are preparing for me in eternity.

In Jesus name, I pray. Amen.